LOVE INSPIRED

INSPIRATIONAL ROMANCE

She'll have to choose love or the land this holiday season...

An Amish Christmas Inheritance

VIRGINIA WISE

LARGER PRINT

"I came to apologize… And bring a peace offering."

Katie held up the basket. "In the form of lunch. The way to a man's heart is through his stomach, *ya*?" Her face instantly flushed red. "I didn't mean… That is, I'm not trying to… I didn't mean to suggest…"

Levi gave her a smile. He would forgive her, of course. In fact, he already had. But that didn't mean he was going to let her off easily.

"You didn't mean to suggest that you're trying to win my heart?"

Katie sucked in her breath. "No. It's just an expression."

"An expression about winning a man's heart."

"*Ya*. I mean, no. I mean…" She cleared her throat and shoved the basket toward him. "Let's eat."

Levi chuckled and took the basket.

"I just meant the way to a man's heart *as a friend seeking forgiveness* is through his stomach," Katie added, her face still red.

"Ah. I see." He grinned at her. "So I'm your friend now, huh?"

After **Virginia Wise**'s oldest son left for college and her youngest son began high school, she finally had time to pursue her dream of writing novels. Virginia dusted off the keyboard she once used as a magazine editor and journalist to create a world that combines her love of romance, family and Plain living. Virginia loves to wander Lancaster County's Amish country to find inspiration for her next novel. While home in Northern Virginia, she enjoys painting, embroidery, taking long walks in the woods, and spending time with family, friends and her husband of almost twenty-five years.

Books by Virginia Wise

Love Inspired

An Amish Christmas Inheritance

Visit the Author Profile page at LoveInspired.com.

An Amish Christmas Inheritance

Virginia Wise

LOVE INSPIRED

INSPIRATIONAL ROMANCE

LOVE INSPIRED®

INSPIRATIONAL ROMANCE

Recycling programs
for this product may
not exist in your area.

ISBN-13: 978-1-335-58609-4

An Amish Christmas Inheritance

Copyright © 2022 by Virginia Wise

For questions and comments about the quality of this book, please contact us
at CustomerService@Harlequin.com.

Love Inspired
22 Adelaide St. West, 41st Floor
Toronto, Ontario M5H 4E3, Canada
www.LoveInspired.com

Printed in U.S.A.

A man's heart deviseth his way:
but the Lord directeth his steps.
—*Proverbs* 16:9

This book is dedicated to my friends, who have bolstered and supported me as I pursued my dreams, especially over these past two years. This book wouldn't be possible without you.

Special thank-you
to my literary agent, Tamela Hancock Murray,
and my editor, Melissa Endlich,
for believing in me.

Chapter One

Katie Schwartz dropped her battered suitcase on the shoulder of the highway and looked up and down the busy road. This was not what she remembered. Not at all. After fifteen years away, the quaint hamlet of Bluebird Hills was not looking so quaint. This highway definitely hadn't been here during her last visit. Of course, that was a long time ago, when she was only twelve. Even so, she'd expected life to stand still in the community surrounding her great-aunt Fannie's Lancaster County farm. She'd assumed that idyllic piece of her childhood would remain the same forever. She'd come all the way from Indiana believing that.

Suddenly a bright red truck with shiny chrome and oversize wheels roared by and splattered mud across Katie's magenta dress and crisp white apron. No, Bluebird Hills was not the same at all.

The last time Katie had stepped off the bus from Indiana, she'd strolled down an inviting country lane to Aunt Fannie's farm. So it had never occurred to her to arrange a driver to take her from the bus stop to her destination. She frowned and studied the steady stream of traffic. The faces of strangers zipped by, oblivious to her. She would just have to walk along the highway. There was nothing else to be done.

Katie raised her chin, picked up her suitcase and set out. Five minutes later, she was already losing her nerve. The shoulder narrowed, squeezing her between a guardrail and the strip of white paint separating her from cars whizzing by. A ravine ran along the other side of the guardrail, forcing her to march alongside the traffic. The cars and trucks whipped up a gust of wind as they passed that pulled her hair from her prayer *kapp*. A cloud of dust engulfed her. She felt like a bedraggled puppy, abandoned on the side of the road.

The only thing that kept her going was the thought of Aunt Fannie's farm, which could not be much farther now. Or at least she tried to convince herself that it could not be much farther. She could not wait to clap eyes on it again. When the letter had come that dear Aunt Fannie had passed away and willed the property to her—the house, the farm and the charming little gift shop—Katie had been both overjoyed and saddened in a confusing tangle of emotions. But one thing was clear—she would carry on with the farm and gift shop to honor Aunt Fannie's precious memory.

But first she had to get there.

She needed to focus, get to the farm safely and prepare herself for the fight ahead. Because Aunt Fannie had thrown a monkey wrench into the inheritance—she'd willed equal shares of the property to Katie and to some man Katie had never met. A caretaker or farmhand of some kind, apparently. Whoever he was, he seemed to have helped himself to a vulnerable old lady's property. Katie was determined to find an amicable solution that left her with full control of the farm and gift shop. Fannie had been *her* great-aunt, after all.

The familiar clip-clop of hooves against pavement pulled Katie from her thoughts. She almost whooped for joy. She was saved! No good Amish man or woman would pass by a sister in distress. She pushed a loose strand of auburn hair beneath her prayer *kapp* and turned around.

A bay horse pulled a gray buggy down the highway. Horns honked as traffic piled up behind the buggy. The horse ignored the traffic and plodded onward with a slow, patient gait.

Katie could kiss that horse. She picked up her suitcase and jogged back toward the buggy, waving her free arm until the driver nodded. She grinned, shouted out a thank-you that was lost behind the roar of engines and tried to wipe the dust and grime from her white apron. Her once-white apron. Now it looked more gray than white. She realized she looked completely unpresentable, and the grin died on her face. This was no way to make a first impression on her new neighbors.

Katie watched the driver's face take form as the buggy slowly drew near. She hoped it was a little old lady with failing eyesight who wouldn't notice her bedraggled state. But as the driver's features became clear, Katie saw a man with brown hair and brown eyes. A very handsome man. Of course she would run into a good-looking man when she was looking her absolute worst.

Not that she was looking for a courtship. Those dreams had died in Indiana, when she'd devoted her life to other things. She had never had a beau and did not expect anyone to court her now. Not at her age.

But still. The man was very handsome. Katie felt her cheeks redden. Very handsome indeed.

The man tipped his straw hat, and Katie jerked her attention away. Great. He had caught her staring. She made sure to look anywhere but at him as the buggy continued to draw near. It felt terribly awkward. She had to pretend to be distracted by traffic. Then she studied the hem of her apron. Then she spent an entire two minutes retying her black athletic shoes.

Finally the buggy pulled to a stop beside her and Katie could turn her attention to the man again without feeling self-conscious. She beamed up at the stranger. "*Danki* for stopping! I'm stranded, as you can see."

The man nodded. "Hop aboard."

Katie tossed up her suitcase, waited for a break in traffic and ran around the buggy to climb in the passenger's side. She slammed the door shut and exhaled as a tractor-trailer rumbled by in the next lane. "It's been an interesting walk," she said.

The man chuckled. "I bet." He clucked his tongue, and the horse pushed forward. The wheels began to turn, and Katie settled into her seat. She had never felt so comforted by the familiar rumble of a buggy traveling along pavement.

"Could have gotten yourself killed," the man said. "Out looking for trouble?"

Katie glanced up at him and saw the warmth

in his eyes. He was teasing. "No." She laughed. "I was…unprepared."

"That much is clear." He smiled. "Where you headed?"

"Bluebird Hills."

The man nodded. "Me, too. It's just up ahead."

Katie straightened in her seat. She wanted to catch a glimpse of the farm as soon as it came into sight. She wondered if it still looked like she remembered. How many changes had that Levi Miller made to it? As far as Katie was concerned, it was perfect just the way it had been when she was a child. She hoped it was just the same.

"Nice weather we're having," the man said while keeping his eyes on the road.

"Thankfully." Katie laughed and picked at the flecks of mud on her dress. "I already look like something the cat dragged in. Could you imagine if I was soaking wet on top of everything else?"

The man turned his head and studied her for a moment. His eyes were warm, determined and serious. Katie felt herself melt beneath his gaze.

"You look mighty fine to me," he said after a moment, then cleared his throat and looked back toward the road. "If you don't mind me saying so."

She did not mind. Not at all. Katie smiled. *"Danki."*

A little half smile crept onto the man's face. Katie could not help but notice how adorable the expression looked.

"Haven't seen you around here before," the man added.

Katie looked over the rural landscape dotted with Holstein cows and bales of fresh-cut hay. "Where I'm from isn't like this at all. I grew up in town. There was always a lot of traffic going by our house. *Englischers* commuting into the city, mostly. So our neighborhood was pretty noisy and congested. Being here makes me feel like, I don't know…" Katie took a deep, cleansing breath and exhaled. She turned to the man and grinned. "Like I can breathe again."

"Never liked the city much." The man glanced at Katie, and their eyes connected. "Bluebird Hills suits me just fine."

Katie felt warm under his gaze, as if he understood how she felt. "Me, too," she said as the heat moved to her cheeks. She blinked and turned away quickly. Perhaps Bluebird Hills held more potential than an inheritance, although now was not the time to indulge in such thoughts—especially with a stranger she knew nothing about. "So…" Katie wondered what to ask without sounding like she was prying.

"What do you do for a living out here? Are you a farmer?" Most people in the little village of Bluebird Hills were.

"Ya." His lips curled into a wistful smile. "It's *gut* land around here. And hard to come by. *Gott* has blessed me, that's for sure and for certain."

Katie could sense his love for the land by his expression and tone of voice. She shared that same love. "There's no place in the world quite like Lancaster County," Katie said. "And Bluebird Hills, especially."

"Nee," the man agreed. He adjusted the reins in his hands. "No place like it."

"There's a hill past Main Street, a little ways beyond that big pine tree they always decorate for Christmas," Katie said. "Anyway, the view of the sunset from that hill is the most beautiful thing I've ever seen."

The man chuckled. "I know that hill, and I know that view of the sunset. And I agree." He cut his eyes to her for a moment, then looked back to the road. "Never heard anyone else mention it."

"I suppose most people don't take the time to appreciate what *Gott* has set in front of them," Katie said.

"I suppose not." The man looked thoughtful as he watched the road ahead. "I'm surprised

I haven't seen you there before. I've spent a lot of time on that hill over the years."

"Oh, well, I've been away for a long time," Katie said. "I…" The sight of a familiar sycamore tree interrupted her train of thought. She gasped and craned her neck to catch a glimpse of the driveway that she knew lay beside it.

Her heart leaped as her childhood memories took shape and became real again. She clasped her hands and almost bounced in her seat. There was the great green-and-yellow field that ran alongside the road. And the red windmill that overlooked the pond. And the quaint little gift shop, with its weathered clapboards and tin roof. Everything was as it should be. Everything was perfect. She let out a long breath of relief.

"This is it!" she said. "Pull over here, please. I'm finally home!" *Home.* She let the words sink in. She finally had a place to call her own.

All she had to do was deal with Levi Miller, whoever he was. In her imagination he looked like an ogre. He probably had a hunchback and delighted in stealing candy from babies.

"Here?" The man's voice caught as he said the word.

"*Ya.* Here."

A strange expression came over the man's face.

Katie glanced at him. "Is that a problem?"

The man shifted in his seat and looked uncomfortable. Gone was the easy camaraderie they had enjoyed during the ride. Katie sensed something was wrong.

"Nee." The man shook his head, but his expression looked grim. "Not a problem." He glanced at Katie to judge her reaction. "I was just headed here myself, actually."

"Oh." Katie frowned. "Stopping by the gift shop?"

"Nope."

The horse turned into the driveway without being guided, as if she did it often.

"You don't…?" Katie felt herself stiffen. "You don't live here, do you?"

"Ya, I do."

She closed her eyes and exhaled. "You're Levi Miller."

"Guilty as charged."

This was the man who swindled Aunt Fannie and stole Katie's inheritance out from under her? She had not expected him to be so handsome. Or charming. She'd actually enjoyed spending time with him.

The nerve of him. How dare he pretend to be such a nice man!

"I see," Katie said in a flat tone as she dropped her friendly demeanor. She was all business now.

"I'm Katie Schwartz. I guess you just realized that."

"Yep."

Well. This was awkward. Levi kept his eyes straight ahead. Katie pretended he was not there. She knew she had to be kind and forgiving and figure out a way to make this ridiculous situation work, but right now she did not want to. She wanted to pout and shake her fist and make Levi Miller get off her land.

Except it wasn't her land. It was *their* land.

Levi Miller could not believe it. He'd felt like a hero when he rescued a damsel in distress from the side of the road. And it hadn't hurt that she was pretty as a picture. But even better, she had a forthright way of speaking that made him want to listen. He had felt a connection to her during the buggy ride—who else had ever mentioned watching sunsets from that hill off Main Street? She had seemed so sweet and thoughtful.

And now it turned out this sweet, charming girl was Katie Schwartz? The Katie Schwartz who had not been back to Bluebird Hills in eighteen years but wanted to swoop in and take over? He had imagined she would be haughty and full of herself. After all, wasn't she just after the money? His stomach tightened at the idea. What if she insisted on selling out, splitting the money and going on her merry way? He couldn't afford to buy her out, and he couldn't bear losing the farm. Not after he had poured his heart and soul into it. Not after...

Every muscle in Levi's body tensed as he thought about Rachel and the life they had planned together. But instead, his wife had died in childbirth, shattering their dreams. Overwhelmed and alone, Levi had felt like giving up. But then Fannie had taken him in as family, provided a safe haven for his son—and a future. Six years later, Levi had become a part of the land. His hopes and dreams were planted there as surely as the feed corn and winter wheat.

Things were already bad enough before Katie showed up. After a spate of bad weather and a season of failed crops, Levi was struggling to get the farm back on track. They couldn't afford to keep losing money, and he cringed to think how Katie would react when she found out. The last thing he needed was some stranger from the city butting in and telling him how to manage his own farm.

Levi steered the team to the barn and pulled the reins. "Whoa." The buggy wheels crunched against gravel then rocked to a stop. He wondered how long he and Katie would go on pretending the other wasn't there. He looked at her suitcase and sighed. It wouldn't do to let her carry her own bag. He wouldn't stop being a gentleman just because she was after his land. He reached for the battered brown suitcase.

"Excuse me?" Katie asked.

"Thought I'd carry it for you."

"Nee, danki," she said in a clipped tone. She grabbed the suitcase and hurried out of the buggy. Levi noticed she stumbled a little as she tried to hop out while dragging the heavy suitcase behind her. He forced himself not to chuckle. She looked adorable with her auburn hair falling out from beneath her prayer *kapp*, her dress and apron dirtied with mud, and her eyes sparkling with determination. She needed help but wouldn't take it.

That's when Levi realized he was in for a fight. This Katie was not going to accept compromise. That sobered him up quickly.

"Look," she said as she spun around on her heels. "Let's just get to the point."

"All right." Levi was more than happy to get this over with.

"This land should be mine."

Levi raised an eyebrow. "How do you figure that?"

Katie threw up her hands. "Because she was *my* great-aunt, not yours."

"Ah."

Katie stared at him for a few beats. "So obviously that gives me more claim to the property."

"Does it, now?"

Katie pursed her lips. "Of course it does."

Levi studied her thoughtfully and said nothing.

"Well?" Katie motioned with her hand that he should speak.

"Well, sounds like you've got it all worked out."

"Good. I'm glad we agree. Let's just—"

"I didn't say I agreed."

"You said I've got it all worked out."

"I didn't say you'd worked it out *correctly.*"

Katie opened her mouth, closed it again and shook her head. "You are not going to make this easy, are you?"

"*I'm* not going to make this easy?" He tapped his chest to emphasize the word. This woman was impossible. "You come marching back here after years away and expect to just take over? You never cared for the place before and now you have a sudden interest? You think you have a right to it just because of blood?"

Katie stared at him with her chin raised and her jaw tight.

"What about the blood, sweat and tears that I've put into the place over the last six years?"

"As a hired hand."

"As a hired hand. That's all you see me as?"

Katie's expression shifted. She looked remorseful. "I didn't mean… It's just…you're not family. I spent my childhood summers here. This land is special to me."

"And this land is special to me after all these years working it. It's a safe place for—" Levi cut himself off and shook his head. How could this woman understand how important it was for him to keep his son secure in their home, safe from heartbreak and uncertainty? A boy without a mother deserved that protection. Levi tried another angle. "I might not be related by blood, but Fannie was like a grandmother to me. I was here for her, all the way to end. Where were you?"

Katie's eyes widened at the question. She made a little gasping noise and turned away.

Levi regretted the words as soon as he said them. He had gone too far. He just wanted her to know he had been a part of Fannie's life and would always be a part of this land. He had loved the eccentric old woman dearly, and she had loved him.

"I'm sorry," Levi said. "That wasn't fair."

Katie spun around, chin high, tears glistening in her eyes. "No. It wasn't."

"I'm sure you had your reasons."

Katie didn't answer. Her jaw quivered as she

stared at him. "I've had a long journey. I need to rest. We'll talk later." Her eyes narrowed. "And when we do, I hope you will see reason."

Levi didn't respond. He had already said too much and wished he hadn't hurt her with his words. But if her idea of reason was that he should hand the property over to her, lock, stock and barrel, she had another think coming.

Apparently, ogres could be handsome. And charming. Until they opened their mouths and implied that a loving niece had abandoned her great-aunt. The thought was unbearable.

Katie had had good reason to stay away from Bluebird Hills all these years. Did Levi think she would have stayed shut in the house back in Indiana, forgoing all her dreams, if she'd had a choice?

There had been some raised eyebrows in their community over Katie returning to Bluebird Hills to run a business. After all, Amish women were usually expected to tend the home and hearth, not venture out on their own. But her mother had been adamant. She wanted Katie to have a chance to pursue her interests, especially since it seemed too late for her to have a family of her own. When news of the inheritance arrived, the family had agreed it was the chance they had been hoping for and that it must be

Gott's will. Plus, her mother's first cousin was the bishop for the Bluebird Hills church district, so Katie would not really be on her own.

Knowing all this, Katie could not bear Levi's assumptions about her. Her hands tightened into fists and tears pricked her eyes at the injustice. She remembered the old saying *no good deed goes unpunished* and barked out a bitter laugh. How dare that Levi Miller accuse her of abandoning Aunt Fannie!

He *had* apologized. She would have to let this injustice go, forgive him and find a way to live in peace together…eventually. But for the moment, it hurt like a stubbed toe—the kind of sharp, sudden pain that takes a person over for a moment. She just needed the pain to subside to a dull throb so she could face Levi again and figure out how to share the property.

Katie wiped her eyes, lifted her chin and marched across the yard, toward the house. She was eager to see the place again. She decided the best thing to do was to explore. That would get her mind off Levi Miller.

She studied the aging structure as she strode toward it. The white clapboards and blue shutters looked weathered, but that only added to the charm. She loved this sprawling old farmhouse. It had been in the family for generations. Katie's mood lightened as soon as she trotted up the wooden steps and onto the breezy, wraparound porch. The wood creaked beneath her weight just like it used to. A row of white rocking chairs lined the front wall of the house. Katie smiled. It looked like the perfect place to knit.

Katie exhaled with satisfaction. She was home. Nothing and nobody—not even Levi Miller—could take that away from her. The front door stood open behind the screen door. She strode inside and let the door bang shut behind her just like it did when she was a little girl. She used to run in and out constantly, until Aunt Fannie would tell her in a stern but loving voice, "In or out, Katie!"

Memories flooded her as she entered the spacious farmhouse kitchen with its butcher-block counters and wide, sunny windows. The living room looked just as she remembered, too, with its battered blue couch and the rocker sitting beside a wooden crate with old copies of the *Budget* tucked inside. There was a stack of fresh-cut kindling on the brick hearth beside the fireplace. She couldn't wait to spend cozy winter nights curled up in front of the fire.

She headed up the steep, narrow staircase to her old bedroom. A noise caught her attention as she reached the last step. She furrowed her brow. Levi hadn't said anything about anyone else living here. But that sounded like a laugh.

Katie followed the sound to her old room, where she heard a muffled conversation behind the heavy wooden door. Katie knocked once, then pushed it open. A little boy sat cross-legged on the floor, pushing a toy horse and a toy wagon in his little hands. He seemed to be about six years old. The metal wheels bumped against the wooden floorboards as the boy imitated the sound of a neighing horse.

Katie leaned against the door frame and watched the boy for a moment. He looked adorable.

"Hello," he said in a serious voice without looking up. He sounded much older than he looked. His attention stayed on the toys in his hands. "Time to go harvest the wheat," he said and lifted the wagon. "All right," he said in a different voice and lifted the horse.

"My name is Katie."

The boy nodded. "I know." He pushed the wagon hard and let it go. The wheels rumbled across the floorboards until it bumped into the wall. "My name is Simon."

"You know who I am?"

Simon nodded. His expression looked contemplative. "You're the woman coming to take over the farm."

"Oh, well, I'm not…" Katie stopped. Had she really barged in expecting to take over? She let out a long, slow breath. She had. She had not stopped to think about Levi Miller's circumstances or what reasons he might have for needing the land.

"I'm not coming to take over. I'm coming to…share." It was much more complicated than that, but she couldn't explain that to this sweet little boy. The entire situation felt absolutely impossible.

"How about showing me around?" she asked Simon, hoping to change the subject. He looked up at her for the first time. His eyes blinked behind his glasses. The lenses magnified his eyes, making him look like a little owl. Simon nodded and reached out his hand. Katie took it and smiled. His fingers tightened around hers, and she felt her heart soften toward this serious child.

"Do you have a room here, in the house?"

Simon shook his head. "*Daed* and I live above the gift shop."

"Oh, okay." She swept her free hand through the air. "This used to be my room." The Plain furnishings and hand-braided throw rug were all the same.

Simon nodded. "I know. I know a lot about you."

"Like what?"

Simon looked up at me. "I shouldn't say. *Daed*

says if you haven't got anything nice to say, you shouldn't say anything at all."

So he had only heard *bad* things about Katie. She tried to look cheerful for Simon's sake, but she could only imagine what Levi had said about her.

She would deal with all that later. One thing at a time. Right now, she wanted to get to know Simon and see the property they shared. He led her through the farm's rolling green hills and golden fields of wheat.

Katie jogged ahead when she saw the pond, and Simon ran to keep up. "Do you ever swim here?" she asked. "It made the best swimming hole when I was your age."

"I like to catch the tadpoles that live here," he said. "I like to put them in my aquarium and watch them develop into frogs. I catch caterpillars, too. I have three mason jars in my room with cocoons inside."

"That sounds neat," Katie said.

"Yeah." Simon grabbed her hand and pulled her away from the pond's muddy bank. "Come on, I'll show you."

They walked hand in hand to the gift shop. The little building stood beside the highway, exactly the same as it had all those years ago. The white gingerbread woodwork beneath the high-peaked eaves and tin roof resembled an oversize dollhouse. Lots of farms in the area had shops and farm stands where tourists could buy fresh produce and Amish souvenirs. *Englischers* loved that kind of thing. But, among all the shops in Lancaster County, Katie thought Aunt Fannie's quaint little country store stood out like no other.

Katie remembered happy summers spent behind the cash register. Aunt Fannie let her have the run of the place, and Katie thrived with the freedom. Of course, it didn't hurt that she had a gift for arithmetic and could add and subtract complicated sums in an instant, even as a child. Aunt Fannie appreciated that talent and put it to good use. The till always balanced under Katie's watch, even when she had to stand on a step stool to reach the cash register.

Simon rushed through the door and scampered up the staircase in the back of the shop. Katie paused to take in the stock before she followed. Homemade jellies, fresh produce from the farm, locally made crafts, scented candles, quilts, rag rugs, faceless Amish dolls and more. The wares looked every bit as quaint as she remembered. She couldn't wait to take charge. Surely she had a right to the gift shop. Surely Levi wouldn't try to make her share that.

Katie stopped when her eyes fell on a big,

black leather book sitting on the counter beside the cash register.

Simon looked back when he realized Katie was no longer following him. "You coming?" He waved for her to hurry to the upstairs apartment.

She smiled up the staircase at him. "*Ya.* Just give me a minute. I'll be right up."

Simon heaved a dramatic sigh, plopped down on the top step, braced his elbows on his knees and rested his chin in his hands as he waited for her.

"I'll be quick," Katie murmured as she flipped open the cover of the ledger book, expecting everything to be orderly and as expected. Instead, the records were a tangle of confusing entries that didn't add up. "This can't be right," she murmured as she traced the rows of numbers with her finger. Katie flipped the pages, eyes scanning each line, panic rising in her chest. She shook her head, turned back a few pages and reread the figures. She quickly did the math in her head to double-check the sums. It still didn't make sense.

The only thing that was clear was that they weren't selling enough to stay afloat. She looked up at a row of faceless Amish dolls and a stack of colorful quilts on a shelf opposite the counter. The wares looked perfect. What was going wrong? Figuring that out had to be her first priority.

"Katie? You're taking forever. You don't want to hurt my pets' feelings, do you? They might think you don't want to see them."

"What?" Katie had almost forgotten Simon was watching her from the top of the staircase. She glanced up to see his face pressed between the slats of the wooden banister.

"My pets."

"Right." Katie slammed the book shut and pinched the bridge of her nose. "I was just…"

Simon scrunched up his face. "Are you okay? You don't look okay."

"*Ach*, I'm okay." Katie swallowed hard and pushed the book away from her. "I was just… checking on a few things." She forced a smile. "But everything is fine." She stood up, jaw tight, and added, "Perfectly fine."

But, of course, nothing was fine. She had thought her big problem was that she had to split the property with Levi. Now that seemed the least of her worries. Judging by the books, she'd be lucky if there was any property left to split in the near future. There was no way the shop could keep going at this rate.

Simon leaped to his feet. "Follow me," he demanded cheerfully.

Katie tried to keep the smile on her face, even

while her stomach sank to the floor. She had to figure out a solution. Fast. But for now, she needed to give this sweet little boy some attention.

Katie followed Simon into a small apartment. The space was spick-and-span, making it feel cozy rather than cramped. She wondered if Levi did the housework himself. The wooden floors looked freshly mopped, and the walls had a fresh coat of pale yellow paint. Sunlight poured through the windows and fell across a red-and-white quilt folded atop a rocking chair.

"This is the living room. There's nothing interesting here. You have to come to my room."

Katie followed him into a room full of cloudy mason jars and aquariums. "Wow," Katie said. "This is amazing."

Simon beamed. He reached for a jar and held it to her face. "See the cocoon? This one is a monarch butterfly, I think. But I'll have to wait and see." He put it down and picked up another one. "This is a common moth, I think. But moths can be pretty, too, don't you think? They are underappreciated." He set the mason jar back on the shelf. "I like them because they are fuzzy," he said thoughtfully.

Katie laughed. "I never thought of it like that."

"Oh." Simon turned to look at her with a serious expression. "You should."

Katie laughed again. Simon was remarkable. She had never met a little boy who acted like a little scientist before. "I will," she answered. "I will remember to appreciate moths from now on."

"Now," Simon said as he swept the cover off an aquarium, "you have to meet Simon Jr. He's my best friend."

"Oll recht." Katie took a tentative step forward. She couldn't see through the murky water.

Simon motioned her closer. "You can't see him from back there."

Katie eased closer and leaned over the aquarium. A great splash erupted, and a frog leaped from the water—right onto the collar of her dress. Katie screamed and recoiled. She jumped, and the frog kicked its little webbed feet against her cheek and leaped away from her. Simon shot forward and caught his best friend before he could fall to the ground.

"Be nice, Simon Jr.," Simon said, patting the frog's slimy green head. The frog turned his bulging eyes at Simon and let out a loud *ribbit*. Katie wiped her neck with her hand to try to remove the slime. She needed a long, hot bath. Immediately. "He doesn't mean any harm," Simon said. "He was just trying to say hello. He must like you."

"That's…great." Katie tried to smile. She suddenly felt how long the day had been. She still hadn't freshened up from the journey alongside the highway. And now, on top of the grit and grime of the roadside, she had frog slime on her.

"Do you need me to rescue you for the second time today, Katie?" a deep male voice asked from the doorway.

Katie spun around to see Levi leaning casually against the threshold. He had a small, playful smile on his face.

Katie scowled. "*Nee*, I do not. I am perfectly fine, *danki*."

Levi raised his eyebrows. "A scream usually indicates otherwise."

Katie wiped her throat again and brushed off her dress. "I just need to freshen up."

"Well, you don't need to scream about that."

Katie opened her mouth, closed it again, then shook her head. "Levi Miller, I did not—"

Levi held up a hand in surrender. "I'm teasing you. I suspect you've met Simon Jr."

"You could say we just became well acquainted."

Levi chuckled. "Put him away, *sohn*. Katie needs some time to adjust before she meets your friends."

Katie lifted her chin. "Thank you, but I'm perfectly fine. I don't need time to adjust. I'm ready to—"

"Then Simon will show you Pete."

"Pete?"

"His pet snake."

Katie cleared her throat. "Oh. Um. Maybe…"

"Relax," Levi said with a twinkle in his eye. "I'm joking."

"Oh, you were so serious I couldn't tell."

Levi smiled. "That's part of the fun."

Katie shook her head. "I'm just glad to hear he doesn't really have a snake in here."

Levi chuckled. "Oh, he has a snake in here. I meant that I was joking about him showing it to you today."

Katie stepped back from the shelves. "Oh my." Katie realized Simon might prove more of a challenge than she realized. This sweet little boy had quite a few friends she wasn't sure about.

Katie felt much better after a hot bath. She dressed quickly and combed out her long auburn hair. She thought about the upcoming meal as she pinned the tresses into place and fastened a crisp white *kapp* on top. A good dinner would hit the spot. Katie could whip up something basic tonight with whatever she found in the pantry, then go shopping tomorrow afternoon—after she made sense of the shop's financial records. She had not been able to stop thinking about that, and the worry had given her a dull headache.

Katie was surprised to hear the rumble of voices in the kitchen as she descended the stairs. Her expression tightened. She had not expected to see Levi again tonight. All she wanted was a little peace and quiet to unwind and settle into her new home.

The home she shared with a stranger.

Katie tried to force a cheerful expression but could barely muster it. The long bus ride, the emotions surrounding her homecoming and—to top it all off—the shocking discovery about the shop's finances had hit her hard. She wondered if she should ask Levi about the financial issue, but Katie worried that he was the type of man who thought he could solve problems better than a woman. She decided it was best to keep the shop's problems to herself, at least for now.

In the meantime, her mind raced with fears over what she was facing. What if Levi had no sense of responsibility? What if he had been the one to run the place into the ground while Aunt Fannie was too old and feeble to do anything about it? How could she be a co-owner with a man like that? If he *was* like that… Katie didn't want to leap to any judgments.

But it sure was hard not to.

"Hi, Simon," Katie said as she entered the

kitchen. He sat at the table, flipping through a coloring book with images of reptiles, while Levi rummaged through the cabinets.

"Levi." Katie managed a terse but friendly acknowledgment.

He turned from the cabinet and offered a charming half smile. "Well, don't you clean up nice?"

Katie blushed and looked away. She must not fall for Levi's charms. They still hadn't negotiated how to split the property. She couldn't let a handsome face and compliments cloud her judgment.

"I hope you don't mind, but..." Katie wondered how to word it nicely. "I'm sorry to ask, but would you mind going home? I'm just worn out. I could use some time to myself to gather my thoughts. And I need the kitchen to cook a meal."

Levi's smile disappeared. "We *are* home, Katie."

"Oh. Um. What I meant was, could you go back to your place above the shop? Since that's where you live? And I live here now."

Levi raised an eyebrow and leaned against the butcher-block counter. "Do you, now?"

"*Ya.* Where else would I live?"

Levi shrugged innocently. "There's two of us and one of you. Makes more sense for you to take the apartment above the shop and for us to take the house."

Katie frowned. "My old bedroom is here. It's all ready for me."

"Hmm. Of course, it would be easy to move the furniture. There's only the bed, wooden chair and rag rug."

"It would be even easier to leave everything as it is," Katie said.

Levi shrugged. "It's a moot point, anyway. We don't have a kitchen. We've always come here to cook our meals."

Katie had not seen that coming. "You mean…"

"Yep. Even if you take the house, we'll be in here three times a day—breakfast, lunch and dinner."

She didn't know what to say. Nothing was going as she expected. They would not be able to divide the property up neatly and pretend the other didn't exist. They would be in one another's lives every day, three times a day, at the very least.

Chapter Two

Levi had tried. He really had. But once again, Katie's attitude dripped with entitlement. He made the effort to be nice anyway. He had complimented her—which wasn't hard. She was lovely. And her smile lit up her face. When she smiled, which was not often.

She was more likely to frown. Directly at him.

Levi had hoped they could resolve their situation amicably. But here she was asking—practically demanding—that he and Simon leave her house. *Her* house!

According to the will, the house belonged to him as much as it did to her. He sighed and turned back to the cabinets. He would keep trying. Even if she drove him crazy. "I'm making pancakes." He pulled out a sack of flour and plopped it on the counter. "Reckon it's not any extra trouble to make enough batter for three people."

"Oll recht. Danki." She paused and studied him for a moment. "I didn't expect you to know how to cook."

Levi shrugged. "Simon and I have been on our own for a long time." The pain had faded into a faint ache over the years, but that didn't mean he wanted to talk about it—especially with Katie. "Plus, Fannie grew pretty feeble those last few years. I tried to help out in the kitchen sometimes."

Katie's expression tightened. Levi realized he had said the wrong thing. She probably thought he'd brought up Fannie's last years to point out that Katie had not been here. Great. Just when they were beginning to have a civil conversation, he said something to set her off again. He felt he couldn't win when it came to Katie Schwartz.

"Don't let *Daed* fool you," Simon piped up from where he was sitting at the table, coloring his book of reptiles. "He can't cook much besides pancakes." He set down his crayon, picked up another one, then added, "We eat a lot of pancakes."

Katie smiled at Simon, but her expression looked strained. *Ya*, Levi thought, he'd definitely said the wrong thing.

Katie looked away, her eyes landing on the fruit basket on the counter. "I'll make lemonade."

Levi couldn't help himself. "It's always a good thing to do."

"*Ya.* I usually keep a pitcher of lemonade in my refrigerator."

"I meant… Never mind." She hadn't caught his joke. He really did wish they could make lemonade out of their lemon situation. He wanted to do the right thing by her. But he couldn't just give up his claim to the property. He had to take care of Simon. After those rocky early years of single fatherhood, life had settled into a predictable rhythm. Levi didn't think he or Simon could take an upheaval. Besides, he knew what was best for his little family and their land. He didn't want anyone—especially a stranger—coming to interfere.

The clack of hoofbeats on pavement interrupted Levi's thoughts. He heard the crunch of gravel and a high-pitched whinny as the rhythmic clatter drew closer.

"Expecting company?" Levi asked.

"*Nee,*" Katie said. A determined knock rang out, and they both headed for the front door. They bumped into one another in the kitchen doorway as they tried to squeeze through at the same time.

"Excuse me," Katie said through clenched teeth. "I am trying to answer the door."

"Nee," Levi replied. *"I'm* trying to answer the door."

Levi shifted to the side but only managed to wedge himself against her shoulder as they both exclaimed simultaneously, "It's *my* door."

Levi gave an incredulous laugh—a laugh that was partly to cover the strange feelings that rose within him as he felt the heat of her arm against his and noticed the adorable look of determination on her face. He liked being so near to her, smelling the scent of lavender soap and seeing the spark in her eye up close.

Katie gave him a thunderous look before breaking away, stomping down the entry hall and throwing open the front door. Levi swallowed hard, reminded himself that Katie Schwartz was the last person he should want to be close to and followed her to the door.

Bishop Amos and his wife, Edna, stood there on the porch. "I was just…" Katie smoothed her apron and forced a smile.

At least she has the decency to act flustered, Levi thought. Little had she known the bishop was within earshot while she was being so snippy. Of course, Levi wasn't being too easygoing himself, but he had been provoked. Surely the bishop would see that. A small, nagging feeling argued otherwise, but Levi chose to ignore it.

"Won't you come in?" Katie asked as soon as she gathered herself. "It's *wunderbaar* to see you again."

"Ya, ya!" Bishop Amos said with an enthusiastic nod. He was a small, fine-boned man with round, red cheeks and a pointy nose. He had always reminded Levi of a jovial gnome.

"Aren't you all grown-up!" Edna said as she bustled inside. She was plump and energetic, taller than her husband, and carried an air of cheerful authority. She clasped Katie in a firm hug—which seemed to catch Katie off guard—then gave Levi a hug for good measure. "I haven't seen this girl since she was, what, about this high?" Edna lifted her hand to the height of Katie's elbow. "Not since we were in Indiana for Cousin Micah's wedding. You must barely remember us."

"Cousin Micah's wedding was a long time ago, but I do recognize you."

Edna patted Katie's arm. "We have all the time in the world to get to know one another better now that you've moved to Bluebird Hills. Never could get back out to Indiana very often."

"Mamm told me you'd be looking out for me," Katie replied. "She sends her love."

Edna gave a decisive nod. "And we certainly

will be looking out for you. You won't be on your own here, for sure and certain. We don't send young women out in the world to fend for themselves like the *Englisch*." Her attention shifted to Levi, and her expression hardened as she studied his face. "What's the matter, Levi?" Edna's hands moved to her ample hips as she stared at Levi with an expression that showed she already knew the answer.

"Uh, nothing." Levi took a step back and rubbed the back of his neck. "Long day is all…"

Amos and Edna exchanged a look. "Seems we came at the right time," Edna murmured. The couple turned their attention back to Levi and Katie, and Edna added, "We suspected this wouldn't be easy on you two."

"Let's talk," Bishop Amos said, the twinkle in his eye fading to something much more serious.

Levi swallowed hard. "Talk about…"

Edna clicked her tongue. "How to share this property, of course. Can't have you both living under the same roof."

"*Nee!* Of course not." He shook his head. "That was never—"

Katie looked mortified. "I would never live under the same roof with a man, and especially not with *him*!"

Edna lifted her eyebrows at Katie's raised voice.

Katie glanced at Levi, then back at Edna with a panicked expression. "I just… I mean…" She threw up her hands. "Well, this can't possibly work!"

Amos ran his fingers through his long white beard. "What can't work, exactly?"

"Sharing the farm and gift shop with him. He's too impossible! Not to mention the living situation."

"Hmm." Amos kept stroking his beard. "It's certainly unorthodox, but Fannie must have had a reason for splitting the inheritance the way she did, ain't so? She was a wise woman, even if her mind did begin to slip a little toward the end."

Katie looked as though she was trying to stuff all her emotions and frustrations back inside. She licked her lips and nodded. "*Ya.* I'm sure you're right. But—"

Amos held up a hand. "First things first. Let's settle where you will live. That has to be decided tonight."

Katie sighed. "I was just making a pitcher of lemonade. Would you like a glass while we talk?"

"*Ya,*" Levi said.

Katie shot him a look that communicated that her offer had been to the bishop and his wife, not to Levi. He ignored her. "And I was about to whip up some pancakes. Would you like to stay for dinner?"

"Nee," Amos said. "Thank you, but we're on our way to visit Viola Esch after this. She's been ailing lately."

Levi nodded. "Let's talk out here, on the porch, while Simon's occupied with his coloring." There was no need for him to overhear what might be a heated discussion.

After a few minutes of small talk while Katie made the lemonade, they settled into the white rocking chairs, glasses in hand. Levi took a long, cold sip. He had to admit Katie's lemonade tasted good. He took another sip, wiped his mouth and set down the glass. "You want to live in the house, Katie?" he asked.

"Ya." She turned her glass of lemonade in her hand without taking a sip.

"Is that a problem?" the bishop asked.

"Nee," Levi said. "Simon and I are happy living above the shop."

"I'll live here in the house, then," Katie said.

"Gut," Amos murmured. "This is a *gut* start."

Levi nodded. Now came the tricky part. "And, while you live in the house, you'll have use of the kitchen, the sewing room, the propane washing machine—everything you need to keep house and do..." Levi searched for the words. "What you do."

Katie said nothing, but her eyes narrowed.

"And I'll keep managing the farm and take on the gift shop." It seemed pretty simple and straightforward to Levi. Katie would handle the domestic sphere, and he would handle the business side of things.

Katie's eyebrows shot up. "You plan to run the farm *and* the gift shop?"

"Of course. I've been in charge of the farm for years. Fannie managed the gift shop with the help of an employee. But I figured I'd take that over. I have experience running the farm, so it makes sense for me to run the other business, too."

"That's what you figured, is it?"

Katie's tone did not sound pleased. Levi glanced at Amos with a helpless look. "*Ya.* Makes sense to me."

"Not to me," Katie said.

"Wouldn't you rather keep house? No need for you to bother with anything else."

Katie's face turned a bright shade of scarlet. She closed her eyes and let out a long, slow breath. Apparently Levi had said something wrong. Again. He didn't know what. He was only trying to be nice.

To be completely honest, he was also trying to keep control over the property. But he was used to running one of the businesses on it, and Katie probably didn't have any business experience. Didn't she want to stay home and cook and quilt and sew? He was letting her live in the house without any protest, after all. She should be appreciative. He could have made it difficult. He wouldn't have, of course, because that would be unkind. But he *could* have. He just wanted a little credit.

Instead, she was glaring at him.

Levi shifted uncomfortably in his seat. "You do want to keep house, don't you? You do like to do the stuff women do, *ya*?"

Katie met his eyes with a firm, level gaze. "Why don't I tell you what I assumed? *I* assumed I would manage both the farm *and* the gift shop and you could take care of the manual labor. You know, the stuff *men* do. You do like to do the stuff men do, don't you?"

"I just meant—"

"That you expect me to smile sweetly and cook and sew and wash for you? You don't think I have a head for business?"

Levi held up his hands. "Whoa. I don't expect anything from you."

Katie nodded decisively. "Glad we got that straight."

"Oll recht," Bishop Amos cut in. "That's enough."

Their heads both swiveled to look at him. Levi had been so caught up in the moment that he had almost forgotten Amos and Edna were there.

"It's hard to get a word in edgewise with you two," Amos said.

Edna chuckled. "For sure and certain."

Amos motioned toward Katie. "Katie, why don't you clear things up by telling us what it is you want to do here? No need to go around in circles making assumptions."

Katie nodded. "Well, I have a head for figures. I was very *gut* at balancing the till and helping *Aenti* Fannie with the books when I was a child. There is no way I'm going to hide out in the house all day while Levi takes control of everything. It's ridiculous for him to assume that he would manage both. Why shouldn't *I* manage both?"

"Okay." Levi raised his hands in surrender. "Okay. I'm sorry. I didn't mean to offend you. I just didn't expect...you know." Levi shrugged.

Katie's eyes narrowed. "For me to have a head on my shoulders?"

Levi exhaled through his teeth. "I didn't mean it that way."

"Didn't you?"

"Let's keep things a little less heated, *ya?*" Edna broke in.

Levi tried to soften his voice. "I just wasn't prepared for Katie to want to manage a business. Rachel—" He cut himself off. That was the last place he wanted to go right now. "I guess I've never known a woman like you."

"I'll take that as a compliment," Katie responded.

Levi didn't know what to say. Was he so wrong to assume she wanted to do the things the women he knew wanted to do? He scratched his head. There was nothing wrong with liking to cook or sew. "How about a compromise?"

Katie frowned. "I have a feeling *compromise* is code for I get the domestic chores and you get the business."

The bishop held up his hand before Levi could counter Katie's accusation. "This bickering has got to stop. Do you think Fannie wanted the two of you to fight over the property like this?"

"Nee," he muttered. Levi felt a jolt of shame.

Katie looked down at her lap and shook her head. *"Nee."*

"Ah!" Amos said. "So you two *can* agree on *something.*"

The bishop's wife chuckled.

Amos rocked in his chair as he stroked his beard. "I'm stepping in to settle the matter. For now, Katie will run the gift shop, since that's what she has a heart for. Levi will keep running the farm, since that's already his job. That splits things fifty-fifty, more or less. Levi can use the farmhouse kitchen to cook meals, but the rest of the house will be Katie's private living space. Levi and Simon will sleep in their apartment above the gift shop while Katie sleeps in the house."

Katie looked up and met Levi's eyes. She gave a slight nod.

"Ya," Katie said. "I can do that."

"Okay," Levi said. "That sounds fair."

"Gut," Amos said. "But there's more."

Katie and Levi both shifted their attention to Amos with expressions of concern.

"Since you're not willing to work together, Katie has to demonstrate that she can handle the shop on her own, and Levi has to prove he can manage the farm on his own. Whoever does better managing their side of the business will take control over the entire property. The other will remain a silent partner. He or she will have a right to half the proceeds but won't have control over the management." Amos paused and tapped his finger against the arm of his rocking chair. "That is, unless you find a way to manage the property together." The bishop did not look optimistic about that. "Sharing control would be the better solution. But since you can't agree on anything, one of you has to take control to stop the fighting."

"Are you saying this is a contest?" Levi asked. He didn't like competition, but he sure wouldn't back down from fighting for his land.

"I wouldn't put it that way, exactly." Amos sighed and ran his fingers through his beard. "It's more of a last resort. I can't think of any other way to divide the property fairly." He shrugged. "It makes sense that the control should go to the one who can manage it better."

A few days ago, Levi had been happily working the farm. Now, out of nowhere, he was pitted against a stranger for control of the property he had managed for years and had expected to inherit free and clear. Fannie had never mentioned there would be strings attached. All his plans for the future were suddenly at stake.

"You have until Christmas," Amos added with an air of finality. "If you can't agree to these terms, you'll have to put the property on the market and split any profit from the sale."

Levi felt his gut clench. Christmas was only two months away. How could he get the farm back on track by then?

"I, uh…" Levi shifted in his seat as he tried to form the words. "I appreciate your help, but…" He shook his head. "I can't part with this land."

Amos raised his hands in a gesture of helplessness. "Our church district can't have this kind of conflict. If you're still at odds by Christmas—or if you disagree with my decision regarding who gets control—you'll have to sell, for your own good and for the good of the community. This is no way for Amish folk to live. If you can't resolve your differences, Katie will go back to Indiana, where her family will be happy to have her. Levi, you're a hard worker and won't have trouble getting hired elsewhere."

Levi and Katie both stared at him.

The bishop stood up and adjusted his straw hat. "Glad this is settled."

Levi and Katie rose to their feet.

"Because my decision is final," Amos said, "now, you two shake on it."

Katie hesitated, then held out her hand. Levi was surprised by her firm grip as his fingers closed around hers. He was even more surprised that he felt drawn to the softness of her warm skin. He tried not to think about that. Thoughts like that would get him off track. He had to stay focused on one thing—keeping control of his land.

Katie marched through the door of the gift shop at 7:00 a.m. sharp the next morning, ready to get down to business. She was not afraid of a challenge. In fact, she thrived under a deadline.

But she had never run a shop before—she had only helped out by doing the arithmetic—and had no idea what she was actually doing. Worse than that, the shop's finances were in shambles, so it would certainly be an uphill battle.

The truth was, beneath all her bravado and competitive spirit, Katie was terrified of failing. She always had been. But she didn't want anyone to know that—especially Levi.

So Katie shoved her fears aside, straightened her shoulders and marched toward the counter where she had left the black ledger book.

"Hello?" a woman's voice asked from the back of the shop.

"Hello!" Katie answered enthusiastically.

She heard a shuffling noise. "We're not open yet. You'll have to come back in an hour," the voice said in a curt, no-nonsense tone.

"It's me, Katie Schwartz."

Footsteps hurried across the wooden floorboards, and a woman appeared from behind the display shelves. She wore glasses with big, round frames and kept her hands clasped together. Her homemade purple dress and white prayer *kapp* looked neatly pressed. Everything about her seemed carefully put together. "I'm Eliza Zook." She pushed the glasses up the bridge of her nose. Katie guessed Eliza was relatively young, midtwenties probably, but she had the prim manner of a much older woman.

"You must be the employee Levi mentioned."

"Ya."

"It's good to meet you."

Katie waited for Eliza to respond, but the woman just stared at her. "I had a look at the books yesterday," Katie said after a long, awkward pause.

Eliza did not answer.

"Do you… know anything about that?"

Eliza's brow furrowed. "About the books?"

"Ya."

Eliza's frown deepened. "Not really. Fannie always handled the finances. She liked being in control of the shop."

Katie could envision that. Fannie had her weaknesses, and not wanting to hand the books over to someone else—even when her mind began to slip—would certainly have been one of them. Katie had to admit she was like her aunt in that regard. "Did Levi ever help with the shop? Does he know…" Katie considered her words carefully. "Does he know what's in the books?"

Eliza's mouth twitched into a smile. She seemed to think the suggestion was humorous.

"*Ach*, no. Levi's not the kind to want to stick his nose into that. He'd rather be out on the land."

Katie nodded. Levi had nothing to do with the problems in the shop and probably didn't even know about them. That made her feel a little bit better.

Eliza's lips quickly fell back into a tight line. Katie wondered if she had done something to offend the woman. Was Eliza worried about her job? Had Levi told her Katie would take over and fire everyone? She hoped not. She had no intention of letting anyone go, even though Eliza did not seem very friendly.

Eliza pushed her glasses back up her nose and opened her mouth to speak, but the chime of the bell above the door stopped her. Eliza's attention shot toward the front of the store. "We're not open yet," she whispered. "I didn't lock the door because I expected you. But I usually keep it locked until eight sharp. I always keep to the rules. You don't have to worry about that."

Katie frowned. Eliza seemed to have good intentions, but Katie did not intend to send paying customers away. "It's okay. There's no harm in opening a bit early. We can make exceptions."

Eliza looked scandalized.

Katie smiled. "Why don't you go see if they need any help?"

Eliza's eyes widened. She swallowed hard. "I usually let people help themselves..."

"Couldn't hurt to ask."

Eliza's expression communicated that it could hurt very much indeed, but she followed her new boss's instructions. Katie sat down on a wooden stool behind the counter, sighed and opened the big black book she had slammed shut the day before. She heard the customers murmuring to each other and Eliza's footsteps tapping against the old wooden floorboards.

"Do you need help?" she heard Eliza ask.

"We're on our way to visit my mother, and I'm looking for a gift to take her," a woman's voice answered.

There was a long pause. "We just put out some homemade peach preserves and shoofly pie." Another pause, then an irritated sigh that Katie guessed was coming from Eliza. "Just look around. Everything is right where you can see it." Her footsteps clacked across the hardwood floor until she appeared around the corner of an aisle, crossed behind the counter and settled onto a stool.

"Eliza..." Katie wasn't sure what to say. "Are you all right?"

Eliza gave a curt nod. "Of course."

"Um, it's just that, well, you were a little brusque with the customers. Can you see that?"

Eliza nodded again. "Oh, *ya*. I'm just not very good with customers."

"But…isn't that your job?"

Eliza shrugged. *"Ya."*

Oh dear. Now she had to deal with an unfriendly employee on top of the financial problems. Katie stared at Eliza for a few beats, trying to understand her.

"The problem is that…well, it's not just customers," Eliza added in a low voice so nobody could overhear. "I'm not very good with *people*. They don't make sense to me. I don't understand why they don't always follow the rules or say what they mean." Eliza made a perplexed expression. "Everything would be simpler if they did."

Katie frowned. *"Ya*, I guess that's true."

"I'm good at other things," Eliza said. "Predictable things. Like organizing a work frolic. Everyone has a job, and they do it. Simple and straightforward. I'm not good at guessing what strangers want to buy. Who knows what they're thinking?"

"Ah. I see." Katie thought of Levi Miller and all the questions swirling in her mind about him and his intentions. "I suppose it would be nice if people were easier to understand."

Eliza gave a decisive nod. "I'm glad we agree."

Katie wasn't sure she and Eliza agreed, exactly, but it was a start, anyway. She laid a reassuring hand on the woman's arm. "Just try to do your best with the customers. That's all I'll ever ask."

Katie watched Eliza straighten her glasses and march down the aisle to where the customers were looking through a display of hand-embroidered pillows. She sighed. How would she run a shop with an employee who couldn't talk to people?

Chapter Three

The following day, Levi scanned the field of newly planted winter wheat. The rolling brown acres glowed in the slanted morning sunlight of late fall. Everything looked good so far. But even if the crop fetched top prices come spring, it would not be enough. He shook his head. There was a lot of catching up to do after last season's bad crop. No matter how much he worked, he could never quite stay on top.

And now, he only had two months to turn everything around. For the first time in his life, Levi dreaded Christmas.

The thought lay heavy in his heart as he trudged back to the farmhouse from the barn. He left his boots in the mudroom and padded across the living room's hardwood floor in his sock feet. The smell of cinnamon sugar and coffee caught his attention as he shrugged out of his barn coat and hung it on a peg beside the back door. Today was a church Sunday, and, as usual, after tending the stock he wouldn't have time to cook Simon breakfast. They typically grabbed a quick bowl of cornflakes before heading out the door.

"Sure smells *gut* in here," Levi said as he strode into the spacious farmhouse kitchen. The announcement seemed loud and awkward in the quiet room. He and Katie had barely spoken to each other since Bishop Amos's visit the day before yesterday, and Levi felt uncomfortable approaching her. He didn't know how to talk to a business rival who shared a kitchen with him.

Maybe *rival* wasn't quite the right word. After all, Bishop Amos wanted them to get along. But with control over the property at stake, *rival* certainly felt accurate.

Katie stood at the counter with her back to him as she pulled a coffee cake from the oven. "I made enough for you and Simon, if that's what you're hinting at," she said without turning around.

"Not hinting. Just making an observation."

"Don't get any ideas," Katie added. "I'm not here to cook for you."

"Never said you were."

"Hmm."

Levi raised his eyebrows and gave her a look,

which she could not see with her back turned. Otherwise, he would not have risked it. He didn't know Katie very well, but he did know she did not back down from any conflict.

"I had to cook something for myself anyway," Katie said as she set the metal pan on the stovetop and pulled off her yellow plaid oven mitts. "And it doesn't make sense to cook for one. I mean, how do you cook an entire coffee cake for one person?"

"I guess I would have made cereal for one." Levi pulled three plates from the cabinet. "Or for two, rather."

"Not three?" Katie asked as she turned to face him for the first time.

He thought she was being antagonistic until he saw the sparkle in her hazel eyes. Her expression sent a ripple of relief through him. Maybe there was a layer of playfulness beneath that tough exterior after all.

"Depends," Levi shot back.

"On what?" Katie asked as she leaned her hip against the counter and crossed her arms.

"Whether you deserve one or not."

"And how do you judge that, Levi Miller?"

Levi flashed a playful but provocative smile. "Whether or not you give me a hard time."

"Pretty sure you're the one giving *me* a hard

time," Katie retorted, but she returned Levi's grin before slicing and serving the coffee cake.

The front door slammed, and Simon stormed into the kitchen. He was missing one sock and his best-for-church shirt was wrinkled and partially untucked. "Ready on time this morning, *Daed*!" Simon said cheerfully before turning his attention to the counter. "Ooh! Coffee cake!"

"Better eat fast," Levi said as he eyed his son's rumpled outfit. "We're still cutting it close."

Simon grabbed a plate and skipped to the table. "Katie baked this for us to share," Levi said. "What do you say?"

"That I'm glad to eat something other than pancakes or cornflakes?"

"*Danki* will suffice," Levi said.

Katie smiled and pulled out a chair.

Levi noticed she chose the chair at the end of the rectangular table. She had taken the head for herself. Of course she had. He scooted into the chair at the opposite end of the table. "*Danki* for leaving me the head of the table," Levi said before he could stop himself. "Mighty thoughtful of you."

Katie looked surprised. "No, *this* is the head of the table."

"No, no. That's the foot." Levi grinned. "It's a *gut* arrangement this way, with me at the head."

Katie's face morphed into a scowl.

Levi knew he was pushing it, but he couldn't let her get away with stealing the head of the table like that. It would set a precedent. Besides, who was to say which was the head and which was the foot? Just because Fannie had always considered the seat that Katie now occupied the head of the table didn't mean it had to be now.

"You shouldn't scowl at your ride to church," Levi warned before biting into his slice of coffee cake. "Unless you'd rather walk. You didn't seem to like that too much when I picked you up on the road the other day."

Katie shook her head. "You're right. I'd better get along with you—at least until you drive me home from church this afternoon."

Levi chuckled. "I've found your weakness."

"Just until I buy my own horse and buggy."

"Your own horse and buggy? Already?" Levi felt a jolt of concern. The shop must be doing much better than the farm if she could make such a big purchase so soon.

Katie looked away. "*Ach*, well, we'll see…" She cleared her throat. "I didn't mean right away, necessarily." She focused her attention on her coffee cake, and they finished eating quickly. Levi took a minute to smooth Simon's hair and tuck in his shirt before he hitched up his horse, Biscuit, and they piled into the buggy.

Katie shivered and pulled the lap blanket over her knees. "Temperature's dropping."

"Ya," Levi said as he flicked the reins and the buggy jerked to a start. Biscuit strained at the bit, her long mane rippling in the wind. "Christmas will be here before we know it."

"It's only the end of October," Katie said.

Levi sighed. Did she have to disagree with everything he said? He knew they were in a tough situation, but her attitude only made it worse.

They sat in uncomfortable silence for a moment.

"Eliza mentioned her family is hosting this service," Katie said at last.

"Ya."

"So, uh…" She shifted in her seat as she turned to look at him. "What can you tell me about Eliza and her family?"

"Why, Katie Schwartz, are you asking me to gossip?" Levi asked with an impish grin.

Katie frowned at him. "You know I'm not."

"Do I?"

"I should hope you do."

"Don't really know you all that well, now do I?" Levi tugged at his beard. "Could be the biggest gossip in Lancaster County, for all I know. That title used to belong to old Viola Esch, but now that you've moved here…maybe you've stepped up to take her place?"

"I have done nothing of the sort, Levi Miller."

Levi gave an innocent shrug. "*Ach*, well, in that case, what do you want to know?"

"Eliza always makes me tuck in my shirt and pull up my socks," Simon piped up from the back seat.

Levi and Katie chuckled. "That sounds like her," Katie said. "But I was wondering about other things…like, how long has she worked at the shop?"

"Oh, three or four years, I guess," Levi said. They pulled up to a four-way stop and Levi tugged on the reins. "Whoa, girl. Steady now." Biscuit stomped a front hoof on the pavement and snorted.

"That long?" Katie asked.

"You sound surprised." Levi looked both ways, then flicked the reins. "Walk on."

"She doesn't seem…" Katie searched for the right word. "Like the best fit."

Levi knew what Katie was getting at, but he wasn't going to make this easy for her. "What do you mean?"

"*Ach*, you know exactly what I mean," Katie said.

"As I already mentioned, sounds dangerously close to gossip," Levi said.

Katie rolled her eyes and looked out over the pastureland. A distant row of buildings beyond a wide, green field meant they were nearing Main Street. Levi waited. Katie finally said, "I'm just trying to understand. She can't talk to customers. Wasn't that a problem when she was working for *Aenti* Fannie?"

Levi flashed an impish grin. "Why, Katie, if I didn't know any better, it sounds like you're having some difficulties over at the gift shop. But with you being so set on taking over the property come Christmas, I'm sure that's a misunderstanding on my part."

Katie exhaled through her teeth. "Really, Levi?" She gave him a look that could curdle milk. "I'll have you know that, despite your mockery, I am doing very well at the gift shop. Perfectly well. Everything is perfect. Absolutely perfect."

"That's an awful lot of perfects," Levi said. "Who you trying to convince? Me or yourself?"

Katie snorted and turned her attention to the scenery.

Katie was not about to admit to Levi how concerned she was about the gift shop. She couldn't let him know how tough it would be for her to whip the place into shape by Christmas. She did not give up easily, but the task ahead was daunting. She brooded as they approached Main Street but perked up when she recognized some of the shops.

Biscuit trotted past the empty shops—all closed on Sunday mornings—until they reached a brick house with a tidy yard and manicured hedges about a block beyond Main Street. Katie saw a row of gray buggies parked in the yard and clusters of men with beards and wearing black coats and black felt hats standing around chatting.

She felt a ripple of nerves as Levi steered the buggy into the grass. There were a lot of new people to meet. Levi glanced at her, and a look of understanding passed over his face. "Want me to introduce you? Don't reckon you know many people here."

"I, uh…" She didn't want Levi to see any weakness in her. "I'll be fine," she said and hopped out of the buggy before he could say anything else. She glanced around at the strangers making small talk before cutting across the yard toward the front door.

"Katie Schwartz," a male voice called after her.

Katie turned around to see Bishop Amos striding toward her. "How are you and Levi getting along?"

She felt a tickle of guilt at the back of her mind. She really should be making more effort with Levi. But it was so hard when he was competing against her for control over the property.

"I think we're getting along *oll recht*, I guess." She swallowed and looked away. "Maybe we could do better…"

When she looked back up, the bishop had a knowing look on his face. He patted her arm. "I'm sure you will." A sly twinkle sparkled in his eye. "Because you really don't have a choice with Christmas coming so soon, ain't so?"

"Cousin Amos, if I didn't know any better, I'd think you were enjoying this situation," Katie exclaimed before she could stop herself.

The twinkle didn't leave his eyes as he gave an innocent shrug. "I think you might be surprised how things turn out, that's all."

Katie frowned.

Amos patted her arm again. "Go on inside and meet the womenfolk," he said before she could ask any more questions. "They're in the kitchen. Edna isn't here yet—she's checking on Viola Esch, who's still feeling poorly this morning—but she'll be here soon and is looking forward to seeing you again."

Katie wanted to ask what Amos had meant by *you might be surprised how things turn out*, but it was clear he wasn't going to explain. Anyway, she was pretty sure she already knew how Amos's plan would turn out—in disaster! So she trotted up the cement steps, walked into the redbrick house and followed the sound of voices to the kitchen.

Katie's thoughts skidded to a stop as soon as she crossed through the kitchen door and entered a room bustling with strangers. Katie had never been around so many new people at one time before. She had known everyone in her old church district since birth. No one noticed her, and she waited with hands clasped, wondering what to do.

After a few minutes, Eliza marched past with a cookie tin in her hands. She stopped short and spun around on her heels. "Why, it's Katie Schwartz!"

"Guder mariye," Katie said. She sensed the tables were turned now that she was in Eliza's domain. Eliza seemed comfortable, while Katie was the awkward one.

Eliza clucked her tongue. "Don't just stand there. Come meet everyone. Then you can clean up that spill." She nodded toward a puddle of milk beside the table. "My daughter just knocked over her glass, and I've got too much to do to tend to it right now."

"Your daughter?" Katie was surprised. She knew Eliza was single.

"Well, my niece, technically, but I've been her legal guardian since my sister left the Amish."

"Oh, I see."

"Here she is now," Eliza said.

A girl who looked a little younger than Simon cut between two middle-aged women to reach Eliza. She hovered beside her foster *mamm*, clutching the edge of her apron with one hand as she stared up at Katie with big, brown eyes. Unlike Eliza, who was rail thin, the little girl had chubby pink cheeks.

"This is Priss," Eliza said.

Priss tugged Eliza's sleeve and stood on tiptoe to whisper something in her ear. Eliza bent toward her, nodded, then straightened up. "Short for Priscilla," Eliza said.

"That's a pretty name," Katie said. Priss beamed, then looked sheepish and leaned her face into Eliza's side to hide her blushing cheeks.

"Priss, I need to finish getting everything in order for the service. Why don't you introduce Katie to everyone?" Eliza strode away before the little girl could protest. She and Katie watched the crowd for a few beats, neither one making a move forward.

"We should clean up the spilled milk first," Katie suggested.

"I'll get a dishcloth," Priss said, scampering across the kitchen. She met Katie in the corner, where they worked together to wipe the puddle from the floor. Katie had to crawl underneath the table to reach the last splatter. When she emerged, rump first, she realized how awkward she must look. To make matters worse, a woman stood watching, a smile turning up the corners of her mouth. She tried to hide the smile when Katie saw her, but her lip twitched with the effort.

"Do you usually spend church services underneath tables?" the woman asked.

"There, uh, was a spill," Katie said as she rose to her feet, wet dishrag clutched in her hands.

"There usually is," the woman said. She was blonde with rosy cheeks and a cheerful glint in her bright blue eyes. "I've got six younger siblings at home, so I know how it goes."

Katie smiled. "I'm Katie Schwartz. I'm new around here." She felt embarrassed as soon as the words came out. Of course she was new around here—that was obvious and didn't need to be said.

The woman grinned good-naturedly. "I'm your new neighbor, Sadie Lapp."

"Nice to meet you, Sadie."

"You, too. I've been meaning to come by. I told Eliza I'd—" A baby began to cry across the room, and Sadie's attention shot toward the noise. "I need to go help *Mamm*. Let's talk more soon." She squeezed Katie's arm before striding away.

Katie hesitated as she watched Sadie leave. Should she introduce herself to someone else? Everyone looked busy. Before she could decide, a petite, elderly woman noticed them from across the room, frowned and marched over to them. "Looks like you've been forgotten over here," the woman said. "I'm Lovina. Eliza's mother and Priss's grandmother."

"Priss has been good company," Katie said. Priss looked up at Katie with her big brown eyes, smiled and slid her pudgy hand into Katie's. Her palm was warm and sticky, but Katie was too touched by the gesture to mind.

"That's *gut*," Lovina said. "But it's almost time for the service to start. We need to introduce you to everyone in a hurry."

Lovina turned her back to Katie to face the room. "Excuse me," she said. No one heard her over the low rumble of voices permeating the space. Lovina shook her head, pulled out a chair and climbed onto it. She looked to be in her early sixties judging by her gray hair and the frown wrinkles on her forehead, but she moved like a much younger woman.

"Excuse me!" Lovina repeated from her high perch. This time the women noticed, and the murmur of voices died away as they turned to look at her. "This is Katie Schwartz. She's the new girl from Indiana who's come to take over

Fannie's place. You may have heard Levi say something about that, although he would never talk bad about anyone, as we all know."

Katie sucked her breath through her teeth. This was not the introduction she'd had in mind.

Lovina gave a curt nod. "That's all I have to say." She braced a hand on the back of the chair and stepped down.

"I wouldn't quite put it that way…"

"It's all right, dear. You can't help wanting your share, and we don't hold it against you. Although everyone knows how much Levi loves that land."

Katie swallowed hard. "Oh." She frowned. "Right." Before she could say anything else, women offering hellos and well-wishes surrounded Katie. Sadie's mother, Ada, was one of the first to introduce herself. She was a plump, nondescript woman with salt-and-pepper hair tucked beneath her *kapp*. A baby rested on her hip, while a handful of little ones clung to the skirt of her dress. After Ada reached over her children to give Katie a hug, more women crowded around to introduce themselves. Katie couldn't remember all their names afterward, but their genuine smiles and warm handshakes stayed with her.

Soon it was time to take a seat in the living room, where the men had arranged rows of backless wooden benches for the service. It was a tight squeeze, but like many Amish houses, the room had been specially designed to be long enough to accommodate the crowd. It also helped that the room was sparsely furnished. The men had no trouble clearing out the three wooden chairs, quilting rack and embroidered ottoman to make way for the benches.

Edna hurried into the room at the last minute and slid onto the bench beside Katie. She patted Katie's knee and smiled. "I'm sorry I couldn't be here earlier, but I'm sure Lovina took care of introducing you."

Katie chuckled. "You could say that."

Edna winked. Like any church district, this one had some eccentric people, but Katie sensed that Lovina and Eliza meant well. Getting along with people like that was part of life anywhere. That realization brought her attitude toward Levi to mind. She peeked over at the men's section, accidently made eye contact with him and quickly averted her eyes. She hoped he didn't think she was looking at him or thinking about him. Of course, she had been doing both—but he didn't need to know that.

Katie felt her tension ease as the service began. The songs were the same as the ones she had grown up singing and suddenly, as the first notes took shape, she didn't feel as if strangers surrounded her anymore. They were connected through a shared faith stronger than any of the differences between them.

No one came into the shop the next morning. By lunch, a slow sinking feeling took over Katie. By midafternoon, that feeling had evolved into despair. Eliza sat primly behind the register, pushing her glasses up her nose, waiting for customers that never appeared. Katie looked at the figures in the books again before pacing the wooden floorboards behind the counter. They creaked as she walked across them. Eliza followed Katie's back-and-forth motion with her eyes for a while, then asked, "Is something the matter?"

Katie exhaled and collapsed onto a wooden stool. "*Nee*. Everything's fine."

Eliza raised her eyebrows but said nothing.

"Doesn't anybody ever come in here?" Katie leaped back up and resumed her pacing.

Eliza blinked a few times. "Um, no. Not really."

Katie stopped in her tracks. "What do you mean, 'no, not really'?"

"*Ach*, well, we're off the beaten path, ain't so?" Eliza said.

Katie frowned. "*Ya*, but…"

"We get a few people. Occasionally."

"We had those *Englischers* on Saturday," Katie said.

"Unusual." Eliza lined up a container of paper clips alongside the notepad and pencil. She did not look perturbed. Apparently, no business was business as usual—yet another reason why the shop was failing.

"What do you usually do?" Katie asked.

"I straighten things, dust…"

Katie didn't know what to say. After all her big talk to Levi, she had no idea how to boost business. Sure, she was a whiz with numbers, but what good was that when there were no numbers to balance? How had Aunt Fannie kept the place going? How had she paid Eliza? Katie opened her mouth to ask but thought better of it. It wouldn't do to show Eliza how worried she was about paying her salary.

In fact, she shouldn't show how worried she was at all. She owned the shop and needed to handle its problems without relying on her employees for support. She had to prove to Bishop Amos and Levi that she could do this on her own. Katie stopped pacing, smoothed the front of her apron and forced a smile. "So, what would you normally be doing now?"

Eliza gave her a quizzical look. "Sitting here…at the cash register."

Katie scanned the shelves of merchandise. "Anything else?"

"Well, it's past time to get the Christmas stock in. Fannie would have done that by now."

Katie frowned. She should have known that. "Of course. It's almost November." How was she going to turn the gift shop around when she didn't even know the basics?

"I could get started on that, if you'd like."

"*Ya.* Please." Because Katie did not know the first thing about ordering stock. She didn't even know where it came from.

Katie walked down an aisle to study the merchandise while she gathered her thoughts. A row of faceless Amish dolls sat on a shelf alongside a collection of pumpkin-scented candles. She browsed the rows of canned goods and handmade quilts. Katie had a lot to consider. How much should she invest in Christmas items when the shop was attracting so few customers? Would business pick up during the holiday season? She would have to study the Christmas sale figures from recent years before making any decisions.

"I'm going to brew us some *kaffi*," Katie said. "It's going to be a long afternoon."

After determining a budget, Katie still had plenty of unanswered questions. She spent hours agonizing over what to order after Eliza explained the process and gave her the wholesale catalogs. As she flipped through the pages, Katie was baffled by what *Englischers* would even want for Christmas. Like many Amish, her church district in Indiana had allowed some simple Christmas decorations. But this did not extend beyond sprigs of holly, evergreen branches and candles in the window. They only exchanged simple gifts, many of which were homemade. Someone might get a store-bought game such as Dutch Blitz or Scrabble, or something practical, like a new set of dish towels or a tool kit. But the *Englisch* bought all kinds of things to give as gifts—even things they didn't need. This concept perplexed Katie.

"I just don't know what to do," Katie finally admitted to Eliza. "I thought this would all be simple and straightforward. It seemed like it when I was a *youngie*. But I guess I never saw all the work *Aenti* Fannie did behind the scenes.

Eliza pushed her glasses up the bridge of her nose. "Fannie didn't get it right the last few seasons, so I don't know what will work, either."

Katie sighed. "We'll just have to do the best we can."

Eliza patted Katie's hand where it rested on the counter. "It's all right if we get it wrong.

There's always next time. We'll learn from our mistakes."

Katie cleared her throat. It appeared to be common knowledge that Katie and Levi were rivals for the farm, but she didn't think Eliza knew that Bishop Amos had put a deadline in place that would hand control over to Levi if Katie didn't get things right the first time. She considered her words carefully. "What if we don't get a second chance?"

"Then we would have to get it right the first time, obviously," Eliza said matter-of-factly.

A surge of anxiety swept through Katie. After all her bravado, she might not be able to prove that she deserved to manage the gift shop.

Even worse, what if she didn't actually deserve to manage it?

Chapter Four

Katie couldn't sleep that night. She huddled in bed, listening to unfamiliar noises outside her window. A floorboard creaked nearby, and she bolted upright. She knew old houses settled in the night, but that didn't stop her heart from jumping into her throat. She fumbled to light the kerosene lantern, then pulled the covers up to her chin. The heavy quilt made her feel a little safer.

Until an owl screeched. The high-pitched wail startled her so much that she jumped up. "It's just an owl," Katie said out loud. She had never been so jumpy before. But she had never spent her nights alone in a big, empty house before, either. Katie was used to sharing a room with two sisters while more slept down the hall. She had not realized how lonely she would feel spending her nights alone.

Katie carried the lantern to the window and tried to make out Levi's apartment across the farmyard. But all she saw was the reflection of the flickering flame and her own pale face in the glass. Katie frowned when she realized her first instinct had been to look for Levi. The thought of him being nearby felt unexpectedly comforting. For all his stubbornness, he had a steady, calming presence that she had not appreciated before.

If we weren't pitted against one another, would things be different between us? Images flashed through Katie's mind: Levi's teasing smile, his gentle tone as he spoke to Simon, the amusement in his eyes when she challenged him. If only he would let her have control over the property, they could be friends.

Katie shook her head. Levi would say that *she* was the one who needed to step aside. The more distance she kept from him, the better.

And yet, her gaze lingered on the darkness beyond her reflection to where Levi slept somewhere in the black, lonely night.

When the first box of the new Christmas stock arrived Katie was distracted enough to forget her *narrisch* thoughts about Levi. Each ornament and Christmas decoration brought a smile to her lips and warmed her heart with memories of childhood. Her favorite item was a framed cross stich that read, "And there were in the same country shepherds abiding in the field, keeping watch over their flock by night. And, lo, the angel of the Lord came upon them, and the glory of the Lord shone about them." A flock of sheep surrounded by poinsettia flowers was depicted beneath the Bible verse.

The red-and-green Christmas quilts—each one lovingly stitched by Amish hands—felt soft and warm beneath her fingers as she folded and stacked them beside a display of hand-knitted sweaters. Katie stopped to smell each scented Christmas candle before arranging them on the shelves.

The door to the upstairs apartment suddenly slammed shut. Levi trotted down the stairs, saw the Christmas wares lining the shelves and stopped short. "What's all this?" he asked with a glint in his eye. "Looks like you listened to me."

She looked up and frowned. "What?"

"When we were on our way to church on Sunday, I said Christmas will be here before we know it." He gave a smug little half smile. "And you said—"

"I remember what I said," Katie interrupted.

"Hmm. Well, glad to see you agree with me now."

"I don't agree with you."

Levi scanned the shop, then continued down the stairs. "Because it sure looks like you're pushing the season to me."

Katie made a sound of irritation in her throat. "You're being purposefully difficult."

"Am I?" Levi asked with an innocent expression. "Then I'll just wish you and your very Christmassy Christmas shop a very merry Christmas."

Katie glared at him as he whistled "God Rest You Merry, Gentlemen" and strode out the back door of the shop.

"That man is impossible," Katie said as she ripped open another cardboard box.

Eliza gave a knowing look that Katie pretended not to notice. Because it was not a look that agreed that Levi was impossible—it was a look that suggested there was something more between her and her co-owner than animosity.

Which was preposterous. Absolutely preposterous.

It looked like Katie was doing well with the shop. Levi couldn't help but notice the sparkle she had brought to the space. The entire shop shone with Christmas charm, and he felt a little bit lighter and happier as he strode through the space and out the back door.

But, at the same time, all that joy made him

feel uncomfortable. Not that Christmas joy was a bad thing—he was all for it. But it got under his skin to see that Katie didn't seem to have any challenges at the shop. Fannie must have left the place in better order than he thought. Meanwhile, he was working his fingers to the bone just trying to keep the farm from going under. He knew that was not a charitable attitude, and he sent up a quick prayer for forgiveness. But he just couldn't help it. Something about Katie Schwartz got to him. She had a way of ruffling his feathers like no one else. She was probably making every decision effortlessly and sleeping like a baby.

Meanwhile, he was tossing and turning every night with worry. Levi shook his head as he headed toward the barn. A layer of frost crackled beneath his work boots as he passed the property's little pond and red windmill. He heard a shout and looked back to see Simon emerge from the farmhouse's kitchen door.

"You eat all your breakfast?" Levi asked. He was trying to give Simon more independence, but his son was usually more interested in studying the life cycle of frogs than finishing his toast.

"Ya!" Simon shouted from across the yard as he bent down to tug a slouchy sock higher up his ankle.

"And you remembered your lunch?"

Simon held up a tin box. *"Ya."*

"And it's got food inside this time? No amphibians or any other pets?"

"No amphibians or any other pets this time." Levi nodded.

"Get a move on, then. Can't be late again."

The one-room schoolhouse was a short walk through the south pasture and up a hill. Simon could get there without crossing any roads, and Levi could keep an eye on him until he reached the schoolyard, which was a good thing, because Simon was likely to get distracted by any little critter that crossed his path.

"Okay, see you later," Simon shouted, skipping toward the south pasture, his tin lunchbox swinging in his hand.

Levi paused to watch him for a moment. Where had the years gone? Wasn't it just yesterday that Simon was a newborn baby and his *mamm*— Levi pushed away the thought. No sense dwelling on the past or on things that couldn't be changed. Simon's mother was gone, and that was that. Sure, it got a bit lonely in their little apartment above the shop, but they had been on their own for so long it felt natural. Besides, Levi knew how to keep busy with work so that he didn't have time to pine away for a partner.

People in the community might cluck their tongues at Simon's motherless state, but Levi had always resisted the pressure to remarry, even though it was expected of a widower with a child. He had never met anyone who could come close to replacing his late wife. When Simon was a baby and needed constant care, Levi had had help from his sister before she moved away to marry a man in a Canadian Amish community. He and Simon didn't need anything—or anyone—to disrupt the comfortable, predictable life they had established since then.

So Levi didn't understand why he felt a tickle of interest at the sight of Katie Schwartz emerging from the gift shop. He watched her shake a throw rug until a billow of dust rose around her like a halo. Katie noticed him across the yard but didn't wave. Teasing her about Christmas must have gotten to her. She seemed to be beating that rug to channel her annoyance with him. Why couldn't he keep his comments to himself? Why did he feel the need to tease her every time they crossed paths?

Or maybe Katie Schwartz just needed thicker skin. Why shouldn't he be free to tease a friend?

Friend?

Katie Schwartz was *not* a friend. Definitely not a friend. He couldn't believe he had even thought that. Sure, despite all reason, he actually enjoyed her company. But beneath that witty banter they shared, Katie was a rival who wanted to take control of the legacy he planned to leave Simon one day.

Levi clenched his jaw and stalked into the barn. He relaxed a little, took a deep breath and let it out slowly. He felt at home here. He didn't have to fight the draft horses or milk cows over how to run his own property.

Except that lately, he wasn't sure how to run that property—and the Christmas deadline only heightened that fact.

Stress gnawed at the back of his mind as he picked up a pitchfork and unlatched the first stall. He patted Old Gus on his thick, muscled neck. The draft horse lowered his head, shoved his velvety muzzle at Levi's elbow and snorted.

"I know what you want, big guy, but I don't have any carrots today. Just came to muck out the stalls." Old Gus gave Levi a more forceful nudge with his muzzle. "All right, calm down now. Maybe next time, *ya*?" Old Gus whinnied and shook his head, sending a ripple through his long brown mane. Then he raised his head, looked down at Levi and sidestepped away from him. Levi chuckled. "If I didn't know any better, I'd think you're acting as haughty and annoyed at me as Katie. I don't reckon you've met her yet, but you will. She likes to stick her nose in everything around here. I'm sure you won't be spared."

"Won't be spared what?" a voice asked from the doorway of the barn.

Levi grunted as his hired hand, Gabriel King, strolled inside the weathered building. He was tall and lean, with an impish grin that spelled good-natured trouble.

"So you'll tell Old Gus and not me?" Gabriel asked when Levi didn't respond.

Levi grunted again.

"I heard the name Katie. Thinking about stepping out with some lucky lady?"

Levi snorted.

"Not feeling talkative today, huh?"

Levi sighed, and Gabriel raised his eyebrows to confirm his point. Two grunts, a snort and a sigh. No, Levi was not feeling very talkative.

"Lots of Katies around here that you could be thinking of. That Katie Yoder is a catch. The one from down near Bird-in-Hand. Or Katie Lantz, whose father owns the buggy shop in Strasburg. She's a *gut* cook, I hear."

Levi sighed again. "Katie Schwartz from Indiana."

"The one who's taking over the farm?"

Levi's muscles tensed. "She is *not* taking over the farm."

Gabriel pulled an apple from his pocket,

rubbed it against his shirt and took a bite. He chewed for a few beats, then, with his mouth still full, said, "That's not what you said last time we talked about it."

"I said that she *wants* to take over the farm. Not that she's going to."

Gabriel crossed his ankles, leaned his shoulder against the wall, swallowed and took another bite of the apple. Old Gus sniffed the air and turned his head toward Gabriel.

"She will never take over the farm," Levi said. "Not in a hundred years. Not in a thousand years."

Gabriel shrugged and kept chewing. "You don't have to convince me. I'm not the one worked up about it."

"I'm not worked up about it, either."

"Oll recht."

Levi scowled at Gabriel.

Gabriel grinned and tossed the remains of his apple to Old Gus. The horse responded with a satisfied whinny, grabbed the apple core from the floor with his long yellow teeth and chewed loudly.

"So what are you going to do about it?" Gabriel asked.

"Nothing. Everything's fine. There's nothing that needs to be done about it."

"Uh-huh."

"I know you didn't see her at church Sunday since you've been visiting your *groossmammi* in Delaware, but just wait until you meet her. You'll understand."

"Understand what? I thought everything was fine."

Levi's scowl intensified. "It is. I just meant, well, she's not so easy to deal with. That's all."

"Huh. Interesting."

"What is that supposed to mean?"

"It means that I met her."

"When?"

"Just now. Saw her outside the gift shop on my way to the barn."

"That's out of the way from where you park your buggy."

"I was curious. And the funny thing is, she seemed pretty easy to deal with. In fact, she didn't strike me at all as the coming-to-steal-your-farm type."

Levi picked up his pitchfork. "I think it's time to get to work."

Gabriel didn't move. "She was sweet as a slice of cake, as a matter of fact. And pretty." He gave Levi a pointed look. "Very pretty."

"Is she? I hadn't noticed."

Gabriel chuckled. "I'm sure you haven't."

"*Ya*, okay, so she was polite to you and she's

not bad-looking. What's that got to do with any-thing?"

Gabriel smiled. "I think you know."

Levi snorted. "No. Absolutely not."

"She's really gotten to you, ain't so?" Gabriel raised an eyebrow. "Makes me wonder why."

"Because being irritating is her one true tal-ent."

Gabriel laughed. "You've got it bad."

Levi dropped his pitchfork. It hit the concrete floor and made a loud clanging sound. "Don't be *narrisch*."

"I'm not the one being crazy. You can't even keep from dropping things when I talk about her. Anyway, if you're not falling for her, then why does she get to you so much?"

"Because, like I told you, she is extremely talented at being irritating."

Gabriel shrugged. "If you say so. But she sure wasn't irritating to me."

"Maybe you weren't paying attention."

"Or maybe I haven't fallen for her."

Levi made a sound of annoyance in the back of his throat, picked up the pitchfork and stalked away. "Time to get to work," he said without turning back around. After that, Levi made sure to stay on the far side of the barn from Gabriel to avoid any more discussion of Katie Schwartz.

* * *

Katie was rearranging a display of Christmas candles when the gift shop phone rang. She still wasn't used to hearing a phone ring, and the sudden noise made her jump. She laughed at herself, then glanced across the shop to see Eliza standing near the phone, eyeing it cautiously.

"Could you get that, please?" Katie asked.

Eliza stared at the phone for another few beats before slowly picking it up. "*Ya?* What do you want?" she asked, then listened with pursed lips. After a minute or two, she shrugged and replied, "Just come here and see. That's what makes sense. Goodbye." Eliza quickly hung up the phone and shook her head. "People have no common sense at all."

Katie groaned inwardly. "What did they say?" she asked, trying not to sound too irritated.

Eliza shrugged again. "They wanted to know if we carried authentic Amish goods. Then they asked all kinds of questions, like what color quilts do we have, are they hand sewn, do we have scented soap, do we sell manger scenes." Eliza shook her head.

"But if you had answered their questions, they might have come in and bought something!" Katie tried to keep her voice from rising with frustration.

"*Ach*, people ought to come in and see for themselves. They shouldn't be too lazy or too busy to make the effort."

"But don't you see…" Katie took a deep breath, exhaled and counted to ten. "Eliza, you can't talk to customers that way. They're calling for information, and your job is to give them that information, no matter what you think about it."

Eliza did not seem convinced. "If you say so. But I really think they should come in and browse. I can't describe everything we carry."

Katie exhaled again. "*Nee*, but you can describe *something*. Please, just try to answer their questions."

"I'll try," Eliza said. "If you really want me to."

"*Ya*. I really, really do."

Eliza turned her attention to straightening a stack of catalogs and papers on the counter.

Katie was not sure Eliza was capable of answering questions even if she tried. "Maybe we should practice," Katie said as the shop door swung open and an elderly woman with stark white hair and wearing a purple cape dress, heart-shaped *kapp*, apron and black athletic shoes hobbled inside. She carried a tin under one arm and grasped a cane with her free hand. "Practice what?" the woman asked in loud voice. She was bent over the cane and looked too frail to manage such volume.

"Oh, uh…" Katie cut her eyes to Eliza.

"Well, speak up, girls," the woman said as she shuffled across the shop. "Hearing's not what it used to be."

"Talking on the phone," Eliza said. "If you must know."

"Sounds fun," the woman said. "I'll help."

"Perhaps I can help *you*?" Katie asked and started walking toward the old woman. "Let me take your elbow."

The woman waved Katie away. "*Nee, nee.* I'm perfectly capable of walking across a room." After a few more slow steps, the woman reached the counter, hobbled around it and sank onto a stool with a heavy sigh. She propped her cane against the counter and handed Katie the tin that had been tucked beneath her arm. "For you. Assuming you're the new Katie."

"*Ya.* That's me."

"I'm Viola Esch. Would have met you at church on Sunday, but I was feeling poorly and didn't make it."

"It's nice to meet you," Katie said. She opened the tin to reveal two dozen homemade gingersnaps. "My favorite!" she said, then set the tin down on the counter with the lid off for them to share.

"*Ya.* I know."

Katie's brow crinkled. "But how…"

"*Ach*, you must have mentioned it to someone. Word always gets back to me eventually."

Katie remembered Levi saying something about Viola Esch being the local gossip.

"Now," Viola said and slapped the counter with a wrinkled hand, "let's practice speaking over the phone. I'm assuming you're the one who needs practice?" she asked as she turned her attention to Eliza.

Eliza crossed her arms. "I can speak over the phone. It's just that *Englischers* don't appreciate what I have to say."

Viola chuckled. She did not seem to buy Eliza's explanation. "Okay, here I go. Riiiiing! Riiiiing!"

Katie flinched at the high-pitched imitation of a telephone ringing.

Eliza sighed, then snapped, "*Ya.*"

"*Nee, nee*, Eliza. That's not how you answer a phone."

"How would you know?" Eliza asked.

"You don't get to be ninety-two without knowing a few things. And besides, you don't have to understand newfangled technology like the telephone to know when someone's being snippy."

"Humph," Eliza muttered, arms still crossed.

"Katie, you answer. Let's demonstrate."

"I really don't need you to demonstrate," Eliza said.

"We can all use guidance sometimes," Viola said. "Isn't that what Bishop Amos preaches?"

Eliza exhaled through her teeth. "Fine."

"Riiiiing!" Viola squealed.

"Hello?" Katie answered tentatively.

"Hello, are you the new Katie?"

"*Ya*, I am. How can I help you?"

"I would like to know why you've come all the way from Indiana to steal a *gut* man's property from him and his *sohn*," Viola asked.

Katie gasped. "That isn't what—"

"I hear you've been bickering like cats and dogs over who gets to run the farm and gift shop," Viola interrupted.

"I haven't—"

"I also hear Bishop Amos has a plan to put a stop to all that nonsense."

"Viola! Really! I don't know what to say to this."

Viola shook her head, sighed and made a motion with her hand as if she were hanging up a phone receiver. "You're not very good at speaking over the phone, either, Katie. You didn't answer my question. We need someone else to demonstrate to Eliza."

Katie stared at Viola as she tried to make sense of what had just happened.

"Have a cookie, dear," Viola said. She picked up the cookie tin, held it up to Katie and gave it a little shake.

Katie didn't know what to do but grab a cookie and stuff it in her mouth. Otherwise, she might say something she would regret.

Levi breezed into the shop just then. He took a look at Katie's expression and frowned. "What's the matter?"

"We were practicing using the phone, and Katie didn't do very well," Viola said.

Katie nearly choked. She swallowed hard and said, "That isn't exactly what—"

Viola held up a hand. "No matter. Levi is here now. He can demonstrate for Eliza. And for you, too, Katie."

Katie shook her head, but Levi just smiled. He clapped his hands together and rubbed his palms. "I'm in."

"I really don't need Levi to help—"

"Briiiiiiing!" Viola interrupted at top volume.

Katie cringed.

"Hello?" Levi asked.

"Hello," Viola answered.

"How can I help you?" Levi asked.

"So what's this I hear about Katie taking your land?" Viola asked. "She's managing the shop

and come Christmas she'll take over the farm
too?"

Levi frowned. He glanced at Katie, then back
to Viola and cleared his throat. "That's not exactly accurate."

"Then what is accurate? She *is* here to take
your land, *ya*?"

"Nee." He looked back at Katie, and their
eyes met. "She's not here to take anything that
isn't hers. Fannie willed half the land to her fair
and square."

Katie felt locked on to Levi's eyes in that moment. She could not believe he was defending
her, as if they were in this together rather than
pitted against one another. Levi tore his gaze
from Katie to give Viola a firm look. "She'll get
whatever she earns, same as me. As they say,
let the best man *or woman* win."

Katie felt a rush of warmth fill her, which she
couldn't quite understand.

"So you and Katie aren't bickering like cats
and dogs?" Viola asked. She leaned forward on
her stool and narrowed her eyes.

"Well…" Levi rubbed the back of his neck.
"We don't always get along. But Katie's got a
gut head on her shoulders, despite our differences. If she proves to Bishop Amos that she
can do a better job, then she deserves to manage the property."

"Is that the solution Bishop Amos decided on?" Eliza interrupted.

"Hush, Eliza," Viola said. "This is a telephone conversation and you're not on the line."

Eliza raised one eyebrow, but did not say anything else.

"Is that the solution Bishop Amos decided on?" Viola repeated. "Or is there more to it?"

"Nope," Levi said. "It's pretty straightforward."

"Well, I guess that's all I have to say. Nice talking to you, Levi. Goodbye." Viola looked to Katie, then to Eliza. "Now, you see? That's how you have a telephone conversation."

Chapter Five

Katie was thrown by the telephone conversation for the rest of the day. She wondered if the entire church district saw her as a villain pitted against an innocent farmer and his motherless son. She was even more thrown by Levi's defense of her. She still wasn't sure what to make of that.

It didn't help that Eliza pushed her to repeat the entire conversation that Amos and Edna had had with her and Levi. Afterward, Eliza nodded and said in her usual, straightforward way, "Bishop Amos knows what he's doing, so you may as well stop fretting about it. Worrying won't change a thing, you know."

While that might be good advice, Katie found it impossible to follow.

Another package filled with new stock arrived at 6:00 p.m., just as they were closing the shop. Katie took the big cardboard box back with her to the farmhouse to open after dinner. When she reached the door, Katie shifted the box against her chest to free up a hand, turned the knob and peered around the edge of the box as she strode inside.

Bam! Katie knocked into a warm, solid wall. Except it wasn't a wall. Firm hands gripped her arms to steady her. "You all right?" A deep voice asked from the other side of the box. Then she felt the box lift from her hands and saw Levi's half smile and twinkling brown eyes looking down at her. "Better look where you're going, *ya?*"

Katie tried to say she *had* been looking where she was going. But instead she stammered and stared at him. Something about his touch had made her face feel hot. Levi looked amused. "So, where do you want this?" he asked.

"Oh, right. Just set it down on the counter."

"Gotcha." Levi strode across the kitchen, set down the cardboard box and turned back to Katie. "Long day?" he asked with that adorable but annoying glint in his eye.

"You could say that."

"Any plans for supper?"

Katie narrowed her eyes. "I'm not cooking for you, if that's what you're asking."

Levi held up his hands, palms out. "Whoa there, just asking." He shrugged. "I was just about to whip up my specialty."

"Pancakes?"

"Ya." Levi smiled. "What else? Thought maybe you'd like to join me."

"You're inviting me to cook in my own kitchen?"

Levi exhaled through his teeth. "Never mind. Just trying to be peaceable. Seems like we ought to try to get along. Or pretend to get along, at least."

Katie felt a pang of guilt. He was offering an olive branch while she was keeping the conflict going. "You're right. I'm sorry."

Levi grinned. "How painful was that to say to me?"

Katie wanted to scowl at him, but she couldn't help but smile at his boyish grin. "Very."

"That's for sure and certain."

Katie laughed. "Don't expect to ever hear me say it again."

"We'll see about that."

Katie rolled her eyes, but the smile was still on her face. "All right," she said as she walked to the propane-powered refrigerator. "Let's get started. I'm starving."

"My buttermilk blueberry pancakes will hit the spot."

Katie stopped and spun around. "No, my cinnamon pecan pancakes will hit the spot."

Levi raised an eyebrow. "Will they, now?"

"Ya."

"Sounds like it's time for a bake-off."

Katie narrowed her eyes. "And who's the judge?"

"Simon. Who else?"

Katie marched across the kitchen, stuck out her right hand and shook Levi's. "Done," she said.

Levi laughed. "Done."

Katie noticed she was grinning as she pulled the ingredients from the refrigerator and kitchen cabinets. She stood on her tiptoes, straining to reach a wooden mixing bowl on a top shelf, when Levi's arm reached around her to grab the bowl.

"Oh, did you want this?" Levi said with a look of exaggerated innocence. "This is my favorite mixing bowl. Use it every time I make pancakes." Levi smiled and walked away with the bowl. "I'm sure you'll find another one somewhere around here."

Katie wanted to frown at him, but instead she felt an unexpected lightness in her heart. Being around Levi was kind of…fun. Which was ridiculous. Ridiculous, but true.

Katie heard the cabinets bang and turned to see Levi sprinkling from a jar of spice into the mixing bowl he had stolen from her. "No peeking," he said and blocked her view with his broad back. "It's my secret ingredient."

Katie snorted. "You're making that up. You

don't have any secret ingredients. You're just making pancakes."

Levi shrugged and grinned. "Maybe *you* don't have any secret ingredients..."

"*Ach*, Levi." Katie shook her head and laughed.

"You can give up now, if you want. Go ahead and save yourself the embarrassment when you lose."

"I never lose," Katie said.

"First time for everything," Levi said as he dumped a cupful of flour into his bowl. He glanced over at her with that mischievous grin of his. "Did I forget to mention this is a timed contest? Better get cracking."

Katie shook her head again. Cooking with Levi Miller was not at all what she had expected.

Levi and Katie each set down a platter of thick, fluffy pancakes onto the kitchen table in front of Simon. "I hear *Englischers* make television shows out of baking contests like this," Levi said.

"Why would anyone want to watch someone cook and not get to eat any of the food afterward?"

"Beats me," Levi said.

"Mmm," Simon said as he tucked his napkin into his shirt collar. "Sure looks *gut*."

"One batch looks *particularly gut*, *ya*?" Levi asked with a wink.

Simon picked up his fork. "We'll see."

Katie and Levi exchanged competitive glances. "We sure will, *sohn*," Levi said.

"You bet we will," Katie said and grinned.

"Quiet, please," Simon said with a serious expression. "I need to concentrate." He made a show of cutting into one of the pancakes and lifted the bite to his mouth with a flourish. He closed his eyes in concentration as he chewed. Katie and Levi watched intently. Simon nodded thoughtfully, swallowed and said, "Not bad. Not bad at all." He pushed the platter aside and reached for the other. "Now for the competition."

Katie seemed to hold her breath. The contest was such a simple, silly thing, but it had been a lot of fun. After all their bickering, it was *narrisch* how well they were getting along. And the craziest thing about it was that Katie's defensive, uptight personality made her all the more fun to tease. The irony was not lost on him.

"Hmm," Simon murmured and set down his fork. He looked up at Levi and Katie with his big eyes—magnified by his glasses—and blinked. "The cinnamon pecan pancakes are delicious."

Katie raised her chin and shot Levi a smug look.

Simon raised a finger. "But so are the buttermilk blueberry."

Levi raised an eyebrow at Katie. She pursed her lips.

"I have no choice but to declare a tie."

Levi and Katie both groaned.

Simon shoved a big bite into his mouth and chewed. He shrugged, took a long sip of milk and wiped his mouth on his shirtsleeve. "My decision is final."

Levi could not help but chuckle at his son's serious declaration. He came across like a wizened old man. Katie seemed just as tickled. Their eyes met as they laughed, and he felt a second connection with her that day. The first time had been when he defended her from Viola's meddling. The old woman meant well, but she could certainly be too direct. And Levi had been happy to stand up for Katie. He had come to admire her, despite competing against her for control of the property—or perhaps because of it. Her inner strength and determination impressed him.

Simon didn't seem to notice the sudden connection between the adults in the room. He was too busy shoveling pancakes into his mouth. But Levi noticed.

And he didn't know what on earth to make of it.

Levi felt an unexpected spring in his step the next morning. Last night's antics with Katie had left him in a good mood. After struggling to get Simon to eat his breakfast and leave for school on time, Levi doubled back to the apartment to switch from his straw hat to his black felt cold-weather work hat. A flurry of snowflakes floated in the cool, crisp air. Fall was fading into winter, he thought as he tugged his coat around him more tightly and leaned into the sharp wind.

Levi blew into the shop with the ring of the bell above the door and a swirl of tiny white snowflakes. The air was scented with balsam and nutmeg. A white Christmas candle flickered on a table beside tins of gingerbread cookies, fudge and peanut brittle. Made by Local Amish, a sign read. Behind a table, a shelf displayed an assortment of cross-stitched Christmas scenes, crocheted snowflakes and quilted place mats and table runners in holiday colors. Fresh greenery dotted with red berries filled in the spaces between wares. Katie certainly seemed to be doing a good job with the shop. It felt like Christmas everywhere he looked.

He heard himself whistling "O Come, All Ye Faithful" as he bounded toward the staircase in the back across the shop. He stopped short at the sound of a sniffle followed by a muffled sob. He doubled back to the counter and noticed Katie slouched over an accounting book. "Everything okay?"

She looked up with red-rimmed eyes.

"*Ach*, sorry," Levi said. "I didn't meant to interrupt..." He eased closer. He had never seen Katie look like this. Gone was the fierce glint in her eye and the determined, raised chin. For the first time, she looked...vulnerable. But she quickly hardened her expression and lifted her chin. "I'm fine," she said.

Levi hesitated. He should walk away. He really should.

But he couldn't.

"Hope you don't mind me saying this, but you don't look fine."

Katie let out a long breath. "The finances are a mess." She lifted the accounting book, then tossed it back down. They both stared at it.

"I thought everything was going well."

Katie snorted. "That's just what I wanted you to think."

"But this place looks incredible."

"That's nice to hear, but what *gut* is it when no shoppers are here to see? Or when I have an employee who can't talk to customers?"

Levi frowned, then nodded. "Sounds like you've got a lot to deal with. Maybe it's been more than you had expected?"

Katie sighed. "*Ya.* A lot more."

Levi rubbed the back of his neck. "Fannie let things go there at the end. Business dwindled..."

"Well, now you know just how bad it is. The secret's out." Katie looked up at him through reddened eyes. "I don't think I can win this competition."

The frailty in her expression felt like a punch in the gut. Levi shook his head. A few days ago, he would have been thrilled to hear those words. But now…somehow, something had changed. "I'm sorry, Katie," he said gently. "I know how hard you've been working."

Katie's furrowed her brow. "Is this some kind of trick? Shouldn't you be gloating?"

"Come on," Levi said. "I may not want to hand all the control over to you, but I'm not a bad guy."

"*Nee.*" Katie exhaled. "*Nee*, you're not."

Levi grinned. "*Gut.* Glad we got that straight."

An almost imperceptible smile briefly appeared on Katie's face, then quickly faded.

Studying the crinkle in her brow, he resisted a strange impulse to reach out and smooth it with his fingers. Or with a kiss. Levi pushed the *narrisch* thought away for a much more reasonable way to help.

"The farm's not doing well, either," he blurted out before he could stop himself. He hated to admit the truth to her, but it was the one thing he knew would make her feel better, for sure and certain. He scratched his beard. "Truth is, I can hardly keep it going, either."

Katie's eyes widened. "What?"

"*Ach*, you heard me."

"Really? The farm's struggling, too?"

"*Ya.*"

"I'm sorry, Levi. I had no idea." Katie shook her head. "All this time I thought you were succeeding while I was failing!"

"Fannie was a wonderful woman, but she couldn't manage it all those last few years. Her health was failing, and…" Levi stopped himself. He didn't want to imply that Katie hadn't been here to help. Now was not the time to pile on.

Katie's jaw tightened and she looked away. "Not everything is as simple as it seems," she said in a cold voice.

"I didn't mean anything," Levi said.

Katie gave a look that suggested she did not believe him. "You think I abandoned Fannie when she needed me most."

"I didn't say that."

"You thought it."

Levi held up his hands, palms outward. "A man's thoughts are his own. Trying to read them only brings trouble."

Katie stared into space for a few beats. "There is a lot you don't know about me, Levi."

"I'm sure there is," he said quietly.

"Are you?" Katie shot back.

"*Ya.* Maybe not when I first met you, but

now? *Ya.* I think there's more to you than I thought."

"I'm not sure if that's a compliment or an insult."

Levi chuckled. "Me neither."

Katie let out a groan and slapped her palm to her forehead as soon as Levi left the room. How could she have let him catch her in such a vulnerable moment? She was supposed to be putting up a tough front so he would know she could handle a business. Instead he had caught her crying. Crying, of all things! What would he think of her now?

Katie pushed her chair back and stood up. Why did she care what Levi Miller thought of her, anyway? She began to pace the worn hardwood floor. Could it be that she cared what Levi thought of her as…a person? Was she trying to impress him with her intellect and competence?

Katie stopped pacing.

That couldn't be it. It *couldn't* be. She started pacing again. This time she was almost stomping her way back and forth across the floorboards. The situation was preposterous. Why couldn't Levi act the way he was supposed to—like an ogre who stole candy from babies?

Why did he have to sweep in with that disarming grin and share a secret to make her feel better? He had put a lot on the line to admit his part of the business wasn't doing well, either. That admission, along with his understated charm, *had* made her feel a lot better.

Which made her feel a lot worse.

Because she could not let her guard down when it came to Levi Miller.

The bell rang above the door of the shop. Katie's heart leaped at the thought of customers. She smoothed her apron and straightened her *kapp*. She was ready to sell.

"Sorry I'm late," a familiar voice said as the sound of footsteps pounded across the shop. Eliza rounded the corner of a shelf and skidded to a stop. She pushed her glasses up the bridge of her nose and regained her composure. "Things were a little hectic this morning. Priss had trouble getting out of bed."

"Is she sick?"

"Only if stubbornness is an illness," Eliza said with a wry smile.

Footsteps pounded down the stairs, and Levi appeared, hat in hand. "Took me a while to find it," he said as he glanced at Katie, then nodded hello to Eliza without stopping. "Turns out Simon thought Oscar might get cold."

"Oscar?" Katie asked.

"His box turtle."

"Of course."

Levi chuckled as he shoved the hat onto his head and hurried out the door in a blast of cold air.

Eliza unfastened her coat and hung it from a peg on the wall behind the counter. "Sadie Lapp should be here soon," she said as she smoothed the wrinkles from the fabric, then plucked a loose thread from the sleeve. "She's bringing in some of her crafts to sell."

"I met her briefly at church on Sunday," Katie said. "She lives on the neighboring farm—the one with the big yellow house, *ya*?"

"Ya." Eliza turned her attention from her coat to Katie. "And I shouldn't say it, but she's a handful."

Katie wanted to ask what Eliza meant by that but thought better of it. "She's a regular supplier?" Katie asked instead.

"Ya. She's *gut* with her hands. Seems she can make almost anything. Sometimes she gets a little too creative, but she's talented."

"Too creative?"

Eliza nodded. "You know, putting too much of herself into the work. Best to keep things simple. Best to remember she's Amish."

Sadie wandered through the door forty-five minutes later, as Katie was sweeping the floor. Eliza was dusting, which they both knew was unnecessary, since she had just dusted everything an hour before. But with no one coming in, what else was there to do?

Katie set the broom against the wall. "*Gut* to see you again." She liked the energetic presence that Sadie brought into the room, although Katie could see why Eliza would be wary of her. Eliza clearly was not one to approve of strong-willed young girls who pushed the limits of Plain artistry.

"You, too," Sadie said as she strode past her to set the crate she carried onto the counter. "Looks great in here. It feels like Christmas has come to Bluebird Hills." She patted the side of the crate. "I've brought everything that Fannie sold last Christmas season." Sadie glanced at the shelves, then the contents of her crate, and moved her eyes to the shelves again. "I've also got original artwork that you might be interested in. I could bring it in, too…"

"This will be just fine," Eliza said. She cut between Katie and Sadie and began unpacking the crate. "We should have everything we need now."

Sadie opened her mouth to speak, then closed it again. "*Ach*, well, let me know if you want anything else." She glanced at Katie and held her gaze. "Something that might catch the attention of the *Englisch* tourists."

"*Englisch* tourists like good old-fashioned Amish crafts," Eliza said as she pulled an off-white crocheted scarf with a matching pair of mittens from the crate. "They come here for Plain wares, not something that catches anyone's attention. If it catches attention, it isn't Amish." Eliza held up the bland scarf. "This is perfect."

"It certainly is Plain," Sadie said.

Eliza gave a satisfied nod. "Exactly."

Sadie sighed and stepped away from the counter.

Katie recognized the defiant spark in the young woman's eyes. It was the same determination she saw in her own expression.

"Maybe we'll talk later," Katie said. It might attract customers if they sold something more creative, but she didn't want to buy more than she could sell. Plus, Katie had already caused a stir as "the woman coming to take Levi's land." She didn't want to do anything else that might bring the church district's disapproval.

Katie went to the cash box to pay Sadie. "We'll see you around, *ya*?" She checked the ledger, then counted out the correct bills.

Sadie grinned. "I'm sure you will. My dog wanders onto your property all the time. And then Simon tries to convince him to stay."

Katie laughed and handed Sadie her pay.

"Merry Christmas," she said. "I know it's still November, but the season starts early when you run a shop."

"Merry Christmas to you, too," Sadie said. "And you, Eliza."

"Mmm," Eliza murmured as she folded the off-white scarf and laid it on a shelf.

Sadie hummed as she carried her empty crate out of the shop and closed the door firmly behind her.

Eliza raised her eyebrows as soon as the door shut. "Like I said, she's a handful."

"What makes you say that?"

"She has *ideas*," Eliza said.

"We all have idea, Eliza," Katie said.

"But not all ideas are acceptable."

"Perhaps not," Katie murmured. After all, Aunt Fannie's gift shop had sold the same predictable goods for fifty years and had never had financial problems until now.

Was it time for a change?

Levi came into the kitchen that evening to find Katie balanced on a chair, reaching for the top cabinet. A cluttered assortment of mugs and dishes lay strewn across the counter. He eased the back door closed as he watched Katie rise onto her tiptoes, strain to reach for something, then shake her head. She set her jaw, scooted onto the countertop and began to pull herself into a standing position. She wobbled and grabbed the edge of cabinet door for balance.

Levi made it across the kitchen in two strides. "Hold on there," he said and put a steadying hand on her back. Katie startled and nearly lost her footing. Levi wrapped his arm firmly around her waist before she could fall. "Do you know how dangerous this is?" he asked. His voice sounded harsher than he meant it to.

"It wouldn't be dangerous if you didn't sneak up on me like that!" Katie said.

"I didn't sneak up on you! I ran across the kitchen to rescue you."

Katie stiffened beneath his arms. "I do *not* need rescuing."

"You looked pretty precarious up there."

"Humph."

"What are you doing, anyway?"

Katie turned her attention back to the top cabinet. "I'm trying to find my special mug."

"Your special mug?"

"*Ya*. The one *Aenti* Fannie served me hot chocolate in every night. It was midnight blue and had a little chip on one side. I loved it, and…" Katie stopped midsentence. "Never mind." She reached into the cabinet while Levi held her securely by the waist. Porcelain clattered and scraped against wood. "You don't think *Aenti* Fannie threw it out? She couldn't have…"

"She never threw anything out."

Levi tried to ignore the clean, floral scent that surrounded Katie. He had never been this close to her before. It felt unnerving, but good somehow. Levi frowned and shifted his feet. He should not be noticing how nice Katie Schwartz smelled or how good she felt in his arms.

"I found it!" Katie shouted. "I found it!"

She pulled a chipped midnight blue mug from the top cabinet and held it up triumphantly.

Levi experienced a strange emotion as he studied the elation on her face. He felt suddenly, fiercely protective of Katie Schwartz. He could imagine the bright, headstrong little girl who wanted the same mug every night and who cherished time spent with her aunt.

"Levi?"

"Ya?"

"You can let go of me now."

"Huh? Oh, right." Levi dropped his hands as his cheeks heated up. He had not even realized he was still holding her. It had just felt right to keep his arms around her waist.

Katie braced one hand against the cabinet while she gingerly lowered one foot from the counter toward the chair below.

"This really isn't safe, you know," Levi said.

He wasn't sure what to do, especially after he had kept her in his arms a few beats too long. But he wasn't about to let her fall. "You're going to have to let me help you down."

"I've got it."

Levi exhaled. "It's a long way down."

Katie pursed her lips, twisted awkwardly toward the chair and tried to reach it with her toes. Her eyes darted toward the floor, then back to Levi. She made a sound of exasperation in the back of her throat. "Okay, fine. I'll take a hand."

Levi flashed a playful grin. "So you do need help."

"I didn't say that."

"I think you did."

"Are you going to give me a hand or not?"

Levi's grin faded into a soft smile. He would very much like to give Katie a hand. He put his hands around her narrow waist and lifted her from the counter. She gasped.

"That's not exactly what I meant by—"

Levi lowered her to the floor in one smooth motion, immediately let go of her waist and stepped back.

Katie swallowed hard. Now she was the one with red cheeks.

"Huh. Seems to have worked, though. You're safe and sound, back on the floor."

Katie smoothed her apron and brushed away

an invisible piece of lint. She kept her lips pursed, as she so often did, but Levi could see how flustered she was. She stared at him for a moment. Then she held up the mug in her hand. "Time for hot chocolate, ain't so?"

"For sure and certain," Levi said.

"Where's Simon?" Katie asked as she opened the refrigerator.

"He's working on a new habitat for his turtles. He thinks they need more greenery in their enclosure."

Katie chuckled. "He's one of a kind."

"That he is."

"He doesn't seem much like you," Katie said as she pulled out a glass bottle of whole milk, fresh from their dairy cows.

"No, I guess not." Simon was like his mother, but Levi didn't want to get into that. "I'll get the sugar and cocoa powder," he said, hoping to change the subject.

"Although I guess, being a farmer, you must like animals," Katie said as she set the bottle on the counter beside the stove.

"Not as much as Simon," Levi said.

Katie chuckled and flicked on the burner. "Does anyone?"

Levi leaned his hip against the counter and watched Katie pour the milk into a saucepan.

"He's so serious and studious," Katie added after a moment.

"And I'm not? You trying to say I'm not smart?"

"I didn't say that." Katie smiled. "I just meant…"

"I know what you meant," Levi said, letting her off the hook.

"The way that child looks at you with those big, thoughtful eyes while he recites facts about animals—it's uncanny."

Levi thought about Simon's mother, Rachel. She had had a big photography book of animals that she loved to look through. It had been her favorite pastime on cold Sunday evenings as they cozied up by the woodstove. Rachel loved to learn things. She was always poring over one book or another. Levi knew she would have gone to college and become a scientist if she had been an *Englischer*. But she had been content with the Amish way of life. Instead of longing for something else, she had wanted to give all that energy and knowledge to Simon.

But that wasn't meant to be.

"Does it?" Katie asked.

Levi realized she had asked him a question.

"Sorry. Does it what?"

"Run in the family? His love of animals and science and all that."

"Oh. Uh… I guess so," Levi replied. "So that

mug means a lot to you, huh?" he tilted his head toward the oversize midnight blue mug on the counter beside the cocoa powder.

Levi could tell that Katie knew he was trying to change the subject. She studied his expression for a moment, then said, "*Ya*. That mug means a lot to me."

"Tell me about that."

She laughed. "*Ach*, what's there to tell?" But then her eyes took on a dreamy glaze. "When I used to stay here, *Aenti* Fannie made us hot chocolate every evening after we closed up the shop. It was our time to relax and chat."

"Sounds nice."

"It was. And I always, always drank out of that mug. See how it's extra big? I used to get an extra-big serving of hot chocolate that way."

"It's a *gut* memory," Levi said softly.

Katie's gaze wandered around the kitchen. "Everything in this place holds a memory." She traced a gouge in the butcher-block counter with her fingertip. "This is where I dropped a toolbox. We were trying to repair something—I don't remember what. And I tried to pick up the toolbox, but it was one of those big metal ones, and it was too heavy for me. I couldn't hold it, and it crashed down right here." She tapped the chipped countertop. "The metal corner took out a piece of the wood there." Katie moved her attention to the windows overlooking the back-yard. "It's too dark to see it now, but you know that big oak tree out there?"

"Ya."

"It used to have an old tire swing hanging from it."

"I had to cut it down after an ice storm damaged the branch."

Katie's attention shot to Levi. "You mean it was still here when you came to work for Fannie?"

"Uh-huh. Would have left it up for Simon, but it wasn't safe anymore."

Katie's gaze shifted back to the window. She stared into the darkness. The only thing that Levi could see through the glass pane was the reflection of Katie's face and her starched prayer *kapp.* "You okay?" he asked.

"Of course." She looked down at the sauce-pan. "I was just thinking…"

"Thinking what?"

Katie shook her head, picked up a big wooden spoon and stirred the milk as it began to bub-ble. The only sound in the room was the hiss of simmering milk, the thump of the spoon and the crackle of the fire in the woodstove. Finally Katie said, "You have no idea how much I wanted to be here."

Levi wasn't sure what to say, because she was right—he didn't know. Seemed to him if she had wanted to be here, she would have been. But seeing how much that old, chipped mug meant to her... Levi's assessment of Katie was shifting, and that made him uncomfortable. It was much easier to believe she didn't care a whit for the old place. That way he could stake his claim without any complications or guilt.

"My father died of heart failure when my youngest sister was a baby," Katie said. "*Mamm* got sick a few years later. She couldn't take care of my sisters on her own. She could barely take care of herself. So I stayed. I always thought I'd get back out here, but it seemed like every summer there was a new crisis at home that I needed to solve. I gave up spending time here with *Aenti* Fannie, but also..." Katie's lips formed a thin, tense line. She reached into the cabinet, grabbed a bottle of vanilla extract and added a few drops to the hot chocolate.

Levi waited. Finally, he asked, "Also what?"

Katie sighed as she stared into the saucepan. "I also gave up walking out with young men. I couldn't get married and leave my family. They needed me. I know *Aenti* Fannie needed me, too, after she got so elderly, but what could I do? *Mamm* and my sisters needed me more."

"How is your *mamm* now?" Levi asked.

"She's doing all right. My sisters are old

enough to take care of her now. But first, they got married, went off to have their own lives…"

"And you didn't get to," Levi said gently.

Katie clicked off the burner, then looked up at Levi. "I don't mean to complain. I was happy to help. It's just that sometimes…" She looked back down at the stove.

"I can see how much this place means to you. It must have been hard not to make it back here for so long. And that sounds like the least of what you missed out on."

"*Ya*. But I'm thankful I was able to be there when *Mamm* needed me."

Levi nodded. "I understand."

Katie turned around to face Levi. "Do you?" Her eyes narrowed. "Do you really?"

Levi exhaled. "I think I'm starting to."

Which meant everything had just gotten a lot more complicated.

Chapter Six

Levi didn't run into Katie for a day or two. He was busy repairing farm equipment, mending fences and traveling across Lancaster County to see a horse he heard was for sale for a good price. Problem was, the horse was a good deal for a reason. After a quick assessment, Levi knew the old mare's days of pulling a cultivator were behind her. So he returned to the farm empty-handed.

He saw Bishop Amos's buggy in the driveway as he pulled in and felt a ripple of concern. Levi had always liked the bishop and his wife, but now he was worried about what Amos would say. Levi counted the days until Christmas as he unhitched Biscuit, then brooded over every mistake he had made managing the farm. No matter how hard he tried, he kept falling short. Well, he couldn't expect to be perfect—that would be prideful. But he couldn't afford to make mistakes when control of the property was at stake.

After stabling Biscuit, Levi found Simon at the kitchen table in the farmhouse. He was hunched over a worksheet for school, tongue sticking out in concentration. Levi said a quick hello, tousled his son's hair and headed to the living room, where Amos, Edna and Katie were visiting. Katie was wrapped in a red-and-green quilt beside the fireplace. She held a notepad and pencil in her lap as she sipped from her chipped midnight blue mug.

"Hello, there," Levi said as he entered the room.

"*Gut* to see you," Amos said. "We were just talking about you."

Levi raised his eyebrows. "All *gut*, I hope?"

Amos chuckled. "Of course, of course."

"We came to see how you two are getting along," Edna said. "Katie tells us that you're doing much better now."

Levi raised his eyebrows even higher. He had not expected that. "Did she?"

Katie smiled. "I did." She swallowed and looked down at the notepad in her lap. "I also admitted that we're both facing challenges with our areas of the business."

"Financial challenges are better than relationship challenges," Edna said with a decisive nod of the head. "People are what matter. If you're doing right by each other, then *Gott* will work everything else out."

Levi studied Katie for a moment. Was he doing right by her? He remembered the frustration and irritation he had felt when he first met her. Somehow, since he had gotten to know her, a lot of that had faded away. She still got under his skin sometimes, for certain, but only because he felt misunderstood by her—not because he thought she had bad intentions. "I, uh, I guess we're trying. We're getting there. I think." He remembered how good it had felt to hold Katie in his hands while she was looking for her mug. He felt the heat rising in his cheeks and quickly changed the subject. "Working on something?" He nodded toward the notepad in Katie's lap.

"*Ach*, just brainstorming about how to bring more business to the shop."

"I'm not a bad brainstormer," he said.

Katie tapped the eraser end of her pencil against the notepad. "I'm just not sure if my idea will work."

"It's a *gut* start," Amos said.

Levi plopped down on the blue sofa opposite Katie and leaned back onto the throw cushions that Fannie had embroidered with Bible verses.

Katie kept her attention on the notepad. "So what do you have so far?" Levi asked.

"I was thinking we could do some kind of Christmas sale to attract people, but that could backfire. What if we don't sell enough to make up for the reduced prices?"

Levi nodded. "I've got an idea." He motioned for the pencil and notepad. "Let me give it a shot."

"Just like that, you've got an idea?"

He motioned for the pencil and paper again.

Katie rolled her eyes. "Okay, fine. Let's see what you can do, Mr. Know-It-All."

Levi grinned as Katie handed over the notepad and pencil. She sipped from her mug as he scribbled away. The pencil scratched across the paper for another few beats. Then he slapped the pencil down. "Finished."

Katie raised her eyebrows. "Already? I don't believe it."

"Believe it." Levi grinned and handed the list to her.

She pursed her lips, then read out loud what Levi had written so Amos and Edna could hear. "'Put up a bigger sign. Pass out fliers. Fix up the exterior of the shop.'" Katie pursed her lips again. Levi couldn't tell if it was because he had bad ideas or if it was because he had good ideas that she hadn't thought of. A moment passed as they all considered the list. Then she said, "I don't want to change the exterior. It should stay the way *Aenti* Fannie had it."

Levi shrugged. "Suit yourself, but it doesn't have curb appeal."

"Of course it does. It's charming."

"It's run-down."

"Don't be ridiculous."

Levi shook his head.

"Levi has a *gut* point, Katie," Amos said. "But let's move on for now. What about the other ideas?"

"*Ach*, I don't like the idea of putting out fliers. It feels so, I don't know…attention seeking."

Levi gave her a look. "Isn't that the idea?"

"Okay, well. I'll think about it. But it's not our way, to seek attention."

"It's not our way to let a business go under, either," Amos said as he ran his fingers through his long white beard. "The *Ordnung* allows some wiggle room for running a business. Like having a telephone or computer in an office. Last I checked, you had a pretty fancy cash register."

Katie didn't respond.

"You can't have any argument about putting out a bigger sign," Levi said.

"I can if it's too fancy."

"I think the only real problem you have with my list is that I came up with it."

Amos and Edna exchanged a quick glance of concern.

Katie lifted her chin. "You think you can waltz in here and solve everything with the snap of a finger? Well, it isn't that simple. This is way more complicated than plowing a field. It takes strategy to run a business."

Levi sucked in his breath. That comment hurt more than he cared to admit. He tried to keep his voice casual and disinterested, but the blood throbbed in his temples. "You think that's all it takes to run a farm? Plowing a field or two? You think there's no strategy involved? No skill?"

Katie squeezed her eyes shut and shook her head. "*Nee.* I'm sorry. I shouldn't have said that. It's just that you shouldn't come in here and act like you have all the answers. It's like you think all my problems can be solved with one little list that took you thirty seconds to make."

"Does it matter how long it took if they're *gut* ideas?"

"Maybe they're not so *gut.*"

"I think they are."

"Fine," Katie said and waved the notepad at him. "You can implement these ideas if you think they're so great."

"Katie," Bishop Amos scolded gently, shaking his head. "Every time you two take one step forward, you take two steps back again." He sighed. "I think what you two need is a change of perspective. Katie, I want you to spend a day managing the farm and see if it is as easy as you assume. Levi, you spend a day at the shop and see how that goes."

Levi liked the idea. He was sure running a shop would be easier than running the farm.

"But I... I... Where would I even begin?" Katie sputtered.

"*Ach*, it's simple, remember?" Levi said with a little more sarcasm than he had intended. "Anyway, Gabriel can help you get started if it ends up being, you know, too *complicated* for you." He emphasized the word in a way that made Katie bristle.

"Levi, that's not the attitude I'm trying to instill here," the bishop said, his tone not so gentle this time.

"*Ach*, I know you're right. I'm sorry."

Amos nodded. "All right. I sure hope that switching jobs for the day helps you be more understanding of one another. Because if not..." Amos lifted his hands in an exaggerated shrug. "Well, Christmas is only weeks away."

"Is this another contest?" Katie asked.

Amos shook his head. "*Nee*. I just want you to become a little more open to the other's perspective."

Levi was pretty sure he already understood

Katie's perspective. And he was confident that this switch would prove all the points he had been trying to make.

Katie woke up early the next morning, raring to go. She threw on an old work dress and apron, pinned her hair beneath a kerchief and set out with a determined spring in her step. She would show that Levi Miller, for sure and certain.

She strode into the cold, frosty dark wrapped in Levi's oversize barn coat that he had left out for her. She tried not to notice the familiar masculine scents of leather and pine that clung to the fabric. The kerosene lantern swung gently in her hand, surrounding her in a soft halo of light that bobbed up and down with each step. The stars still shone in the black sky, and the horizon showed no promise of light.

Katie's breath fogged the still air while her feet crunched against the white frost–coated grass. The chicken coop was quiet as she passed it. She had woken before the rooster, which gave her a sense of satisfaction. She was going to sail through her jobs before Levi knew what was happening. Ha! He was probably still sleeping. Katie smiled as she unlatched the barn door and pushed. Her smile faded as she strained to move the heavy wood. She had not anticipated how much effort it would take.

The earthy scents of animals and manure met her as she wrestled the doors open wide enough to slip through. A horse whinnied, and hooves stomped against hay in the darkness. She raised the kerosene lantern and watched strange shadows dance across the walls as she made her way down the row of stalls to the milk cows at the far end. Their wet black eyes followed her movements as she hung the lantern on a peg and studied the diesel-powered milking machine.

Well. This looked a little more complicated than she'd anticipated. Katie hesitated, then pressed a button, expecting the machine to sputter and come alive. It did not. She glanced at the cows. They chewed their cud solemnly while keeping a watchful eye on her. She felt sure they disapproved of her, then laughed out loud at the silly notion.

"Having fun?"

"What?" Katie startled and turned toward Levi's deep, familiar voice across the cavernous barn.

"You're laughing. Didn't know milking was so amusing."

"No, I just..." Katie grabbed the kerosene lantern from the peg and moved it in front of her. A tall silhouette appeared in the darkness. She could hear heavy, booted footsteps coming closer. "I was just thinking the cows... Never mind." She shook her head. "What are you doing here, anyway?"

"I didn't want you to hurt any of the cows."

"I'm not going to hurt the cows!"

"Then I don't want them to hurt you."

"I've got this, Levi."

Levi's features slowly came of out shadow and into view as he neared Katie's lantern. "Do you?"

"For sure and certain."

"Go on, then. I'll be a neutral observer. Like the UN."

Katie almost chuckled, but she had too much to prove to laugh at Levi's little jokes. She turned back to the portable milking machine and frowned as she passed the lantern over it. With all its plastic tubes and shiny metal gauges, the contraption looked more like something from a dentist's office than farm equipment.

"Gotta turn it on first," Levi said.

"*Ya.* I am."

"Are you?"

Katie pursed her lips and flipped a switch. Nothing happened.

Levi reached around her. Katie could hear the soft rasp of his breath near her ear, which made her uncomfortable. Not because he was too close, but because she liked that he was so close—which was exasperating, since he was being such a know-it-all. But those strong arms were practically holding her, and something about it felt so…comforting. Her face turned up to look at Levi's as he leaned over her. She could see the hard edge of his profile in the soft glow of the lantern light. His eyes shifted to hers, and they stared at one another for an instant that made Katie's breath catch in her throat.

Then the milking machine sputtered to life. Levi grinned and stepped back. "Well, have at it," he said with a casual smirk.

Katie's cheeks burned. She had thought that she and Levi were having a moment, but he had just been leaning over her to turn on the machine, nothing more. She jerked away from him and began to fumble with the hoses snaking from the contraption—anything to distract her from the awkward rejection she was feeling. Levi stood over her, watching closely. She could feel his eyes burning into her back. "Give me a little space, why don't you?" One of the tubes slipped from her fingers and clattered against the machine. "I can't think straight when you're hovering like that."

Levi took a step back and leaned a shoulder casually against the wall. "Whatever helps," he said. Katie knew he had a smirk on his face without having to look.

"You ought to be getting to the shop, ain't so?" Katie asked.

Levi looked at the open barn door. A weak, yellow haze softened the darkness above the horizon. "I've got time yet. Shopkeepers keep much later hours than farmers."

"Are you calling me lazy?" Katie asked as she jerked at the portable milking machine to roll it toward the cows.

"*Nee.* Just stating facts."

Katie glanced at his expression and saw he was smiling.

"I can never tell if you're really this difficult or if this is your idea of fun."

Levi shrugged and folded his arms—he was still leaning negligently against the wall. "Why, Katie Schwartz, I didn't realize you thought I was fun."

"That's not what I said and you know it."

"What I know is that June is never going to let you milk her while you're scowling like that."

Katie stopped short and moved her attention from lugging the milk machine across the concrete floor to the cow in front of her. The cow shuffled sideways, away from Katie, and mooed mournfully.

"See what I mean?" Levi asked. He looked like he was enjoying himself.

Katie forced a smile. "Good cow. Nice cow."

"You know cows are more dangerous than sharks. Statistically speaking."

Katie stiffened. "Good cow," she repeated, but in a much more hesitant voice. "Okay, I'm just going to…" Katie ran her eyes over the machine. "Hook this up to you and…"

"Never milked a cow before? Not even by hand?"

Katie shook her head. "We didn't keep cows. We lived in town, remember?"

"Well, as amusing as this is, I can't let you stress June out." Levi pushed off the wall and lumbered over to the cow. She stepped toward him and lowered her head to greet him.

Katie frowned. What did Levi have that she didn't have?

"Jealous?" Levi asked with a grin.

"No." Katie put her hands on her hips. "Okay, maybe. Just a little." Katie watched as Levi spoke to June in low, soothing tones. She had not seen this gentle, calming side of him before. She wanted to be irritated that he was taking over the milking, but instead she felt strangely touched by the way he treated his animals. Katie's *mamm* always said you knew a man's character by the way he treated his horses. Seems that applied to cows as well.

Except that would mean that the man trying to steal Aunt Fannie's property was of good character. A few weeks ago, that would have seemed laughable. Now it felt obvious. As much as she hated to admit it, Katie had seen too much of Levi to envision him as an ogre who took advantage of little old ladies.

The problem was, she had no idea where to go from here. If he had good intentions, how could she fight him for the inheritance? Her determination to win wasn't sitting as well with her as it once did.

"Levi?"

"Ya?" he replied as he patted June's flank.

"What made you want this property?"

Levi's hand froze. The barn fell silent except for the stomp of a hoof in a distant stall and the hiss of June's warm breath in the brisk morning air. "Guess I've just put a lot into it." He reached for the milking machine.

"I think there's more to it than that," Katie said.

"Got a *sohn* to raise. Need to secure his future."

"But why here?"

Levi cleared his throat. "Simon's mother…" He cut himself off and shook his head.

The barn door creaked, and footsteps echoed against the concrete floor.

Levi exhaled. "Gabriel's here. I'll leave this to him. He'll show you what to do today, *ya*?"

"Oll recht. Sure." Katie watched as Levi gave June a quick pat on the shoulder and then conveniently fled the barn, leaving her with more questions than answers.

* * *

Levi felt confident as he strode into the shop. How hard could it be to push some buttons on the cash register and put things on a display shelf? He'd already managed to get Simon off to school on time and made sure Katie was safe with the cows. Not a bad start on the day. The problem was he couldn't get Katie's determined expression out of his head. She had looked ridiculously adorable lugging that milking machine across the floor while pretending that she knew what she was doing. And when he pointed out that cows could be dangerous, her expression had been priceless.

Unfortunately, instead of feeling a thrill of victory, he had felt the need to scoop her in his arms.

Which was *narrisch*. Completely and absolutely crazy.

Better focus on today's job and get Katie Schwartz out of his head.

"You already here, Eliza?" Levi called across the shop.

"*Ya*, I'm here."

"I guess Katie filled you in on today's plans?" Levi strode to the back of the shop and hung his coat on a peg on the wall. The warm air mingled with the scents of pine and cranberry from potpourri tucked into hand-woven baskets.

"She left me a note," Eliza said, peering up at him from behind her big, round glasses. She raised her eyebrows. "But the note didn't explain why you're working here today. Just that you are."

"Call it a Christmas challenge," Levi said. He slapped his hands together and rubbed them. "So, where to begin…" Levi whistled the first bar of "Away in a Manger" as he took a step back to survey the store. Something brushed against his back. He turned to see what was there and felt his elbow catch on something else. Next thing he knew the sound of shattering glass hit his ears. He flinched and looked down. A ceramic cookie jar lay in pieces on the floor, frosted gingerbread men scattered among the shards.

"You can begin by not breaking the merchandise," Eliza said.

Levi exhaled. "Right."

Eliza stared at him.

"Uh, guess I better get this cleaned up."

He swept up the gingerbread cookies and shattered ceramic, dumped the debris into the trash can, and told Eliza to ring it up. He pulled a few bills from his pocket, counted them out and handed them over.

"Would you like that gift wrapped?" Eliza asked as she punched buttons on the cash register.

"Why, Eliza Zook, did you just make a joke?"

A faint smile turned up one corner of her mouth. "Possibly."

Levi chuckled. "Hey, we've been friends for a long time, ain't so?"

"Ya." Eliza's tone sounded slightly suspicious. She clearly knew where this was going.

"So, uh, no need to mention that to Katie, *ya?*"

Eliza pushed the drawer into the cash register and gave Levi a stern look over the top of her glasses.

"I'm going to take that as a no," Levi said.

"I'm duty bound to report everything that goes on in this shop."

"Everything?"

"Everything."

"You really don't bend at all, do you, Eliza?"

"Thank you for noticing. It's one of my best qualities."

Right. Rules were important to Levi, too—he was Amish, after all—but Eliza didn't believe in gray areas. Everything was black and white to her. Levi found life too complicated for that way of thinking. Sometimes it got him into trouble.

Like when he began to think the rival to his business was too intriguing to be a rival any more. He didn't know what Katie was to him, but whatever she was, she wasn't a rival.

But she wasn't a partner, either.

Not yet, anyway.

The bell above the door to the shop rang, and the room filled with the low murmur of voices speaking English and a cloud of fancy perfume. Eliza's eyes widened. "Customers!" she mouthed.

"Ya."

Eliza stood up, cleared her throat and marched to them. "Hello, and welcome to our gift shop." There was a moment of silence. Then Eliza reappeared at the counter.

The interaction had seemed a bit awkward, but Levi was impressed at how much Eliza's social skills had improved.

"You go see what they want now," Eliza said. "It's your job today."

"Looks like you were handling it just fine yourself."

"Ach, well, it's been one of Katie's initiatives for us to work on customer relations."

Levi chuckled inside. Leave it to Katie to figure out a way to coax Eliza into being more polite to customers.

"But today, you're supposed to handle that. Katie's orders. Now, go on." Eliza made a shooing motion with her hands. Levi strode across the shop until he rounded the corner of a display shelf to see a woman with blond hair wearing a long red coat trimmed in faux fur. A little girl beside her wore yellow leggings with pink hearts printed on them and a puffy pink coat. Levi was used to being insulated from the world, so it felt strange to see *Englischers*. He wondered if Katie felt comfortable interacting with them. He wasn't uptight about it like Eliza was, but he didn't feel quite right, either. He wondered what they thought of his black trousers, black suspenders and plain blue shirt. Did he look as strange to them as they did to him?

"Gude mariye," he said, then quickly switched to English. "Good morning. Can I help you?"

The woman waved her hand over the shelves. A gold bracelet clinked as she moved. "I'm trying to find a little porcelain windmill that says Amish Country on it." She held up her hands to demonstrate the size. "About this big." She looked sheepish. "I know it's a long shot, but when I was growing up, my grandmother had one that she bought here in Bluebird Hills. I was driving by, saw the shop and it just tugged at my memory, you know? It's a sentimental thing." The woman laughed. "You probably don't have it. My grandmother would have bought hers years ago. They probably don't even make anything like that any more."

"Um, well…" Levi scratched his jaw through his beard. "Let me see what I can do."

The woman's face lit up. "You think you might have it?"

"Uh…probably not. But I'll make sure."

"Oh." The woman deflated. "Thanks for checking anyway."

Levi nodded. He wondered where to look. It was like finding a needle in a haystack. He knew the shop carried a wide variety of Amish-themed knickknacks and handmade Amish goods, but he had never thought about how difficult it would be to find one specific item among all the rest. He browsed the aisles, eyes darting back and forth, up and down. He couldn't even find a single porcelain figurine, much less a windmill.

Levi heard the little girl whine that she wanted to go. He peered around the end of an aisle and saw the girl tugging on her mother's hand. The mother looked flustered. "Just a sec, okay? Please?"

"No. I want to go. I'm bored."

The woman sighed. "Okay."

Levi couldn't believe what he was hearing. Simon could push the boundaries sometimes, but he would never tell his father no outright like that. Amish parents were not as indulgent as *Englischers*—and it showed in their children's behavior.

"I'll be right with you," Levi shouted across

the shop and darted to where Eliza sat on her wooden stool behind the counter. "Do we have a porcelain windmill that says Amish Country on it?"

"Um…" Eliza's eyes looked upward as she thought about it. "No, we don't have that one. But we do have—"

"Okay, thanks," Levi said, cutting her off and rushing back across the shop to catch the woman before she left. "Hi. Sorry. Took me a while to look for it."

"You don't know what's here, do you?" the woman said. "It's been like ten minutes. Are you new or something?"

Levi rubbed the back of his neck. "Uh, you could say that. But I asked Eliza, who's worked here for years, and she said we don't have it."

"Why didn't you just ask her to begin with? My daughter's gotten really impatient waiting."

Levi shuffled his feet. He wanted to snap at the woman and tell her he was trying his best to find her figurine, even though it was practically impossible. Instead he plastered on a smile and apologized.

The woman handed him a business card. "In case you get it in. You can call my work number or cell phone. It doesn't matter which." She stopped and crinkled her brow. "Wait, you don't use phones, do you?"

"Our church district allows it for business."

"Oh? Well, lucky for me, then."

Levi smiled again. His cheeks were beginning to ache from the effort. He was not used to making people feel welcomed and attended to. Plus, he was still a little miffed over her criticism. He said a quick, silent prayer for patience and gave a cheerful goodbye. "And goodbye to you, too," he said with a big wave to the little girl.

The little girl shook her head.

"No goodbye?" Levi asked as he leaned down with a smile.

"I'm not allowed to talk to strangers," she said as she scooted closer to her mother.

"Oh." Levi straightened up and cleared his throat. "Of course. Well, good job, then." He watched the two *Englischers* walk out the door hand in hand and thought about the world that little girl inhabited—one where she couldn't talk to people in her own community. He had always taken it for granted that he could trust anyone wearing Amish clothing speaking Pennsylvania Dutch.

After the door shut, Levi strolled back to the counter, where he found Eliza scribbling on a yellow notepad.

She glanced up at him, set down her pen and flipped over the notepad.

Levi frowned. "What are you writing?"

"Nothing for you to see."

Now he had to know. "Why not?"

Eliza opened a drawer, pulled out a small cloth, took off her glasses and began to wipe the lenses. "If you must know, I am taking notes to keep Katie informed."

Levi snorted. "That's a little much, ain't so?"

Eliza kept wiping the lenses in slow circles. "I like to do a precise, thorough job," she said without looking at Levi. "And it's important that Katie knows I'm a reliable employee."

Levi let out a low whistle. "This is going to be a long day, isn't it?"

Eliza chose not to answer.

Chapter Seven

Katie had to disinfect the milking machine after they finished milking, then muck out the horses' stalls before trudging across the property to mend fences. She couldn't figure out how to repair a rotted slat of wood without dismantling the entire section, which seemed like too big a job for her to undertake. It wasn't that she *couldn't* use a hammer, nails, saw and level—it's just that she never had tried before.

Gabriel was not much help—he leaned against the fence with a piece of straw between his teeth, watching Katie's unsuccessful attempts at repairs—and she suspected that Levi had instructed Gabriel to leave all the work to her while keeping her from causing any damage. If so, Gabriel had no trouble following those instructions. The nineteen-year-old had a mischievous glint in his brown eyes, a sprinkle of freckles across the bridge of his nose and tousled brown hair beneath his hat—a rumpled, carefree look that made Katie feel sure he was the type to go along with Levi's nonsense. He seemed like one of those *youngies* who were too restless to appreciate a Plain lifestyle and got into too much trouble during *rumspringa*.

Katie was exhausted by the time she lugged herself back to the farmhouse for a quick bowl of reheated soup, a sandwich and some hot *kaffi*. Her face was smudged with dirt, mud splattered her work apron and her arms were sore. The more hungry and tired she felt, the more annoyed she got at Levi. After all, she had not instructed Eliza to make things harder on Levi.

Of course, she had not needed to. Katie suspected Eliza would do that all on her own.

Katie had meant to hurry back out, but she was still slumped over the table sipping a second cup of *kaffi* and resting her sore muscles when Levi strolled through the door with a half smile on his face that looked cuter than Katie wanted to admit. "Taking a pretty long lunch, ain't so?"

"I was just leaving. And anyway, how would you know?"

"The shop does have windows. Saw you come in here an hour ago."

"So you've been spying on me."

"Just keeping a lookout. Can't have you destroying the farm."

"I am not going to destroy the farm, Levi Miller!" Katie pushed back her chair and stood up.

"No, because I've made sure you're supervised."

"I do *not* need supervision."

Levi looked through the open hall door, into the living room, where Gabriel had taken advantage of the longer-than-usual lunch break to lounge on the sofa with his sock feet propped on the coffee table, whittling a wooden horse. Gabriel looked up from his work to make eye contact with Levi and raise his eyebrows in an expression that clearly meant *she most certainly does need supervision.*

Katie made a sound of irritation in the back of her throat and marched to the sink to rinse her dishes.

"Well, since you've got everything covered, you'll have no trouble doing some repair work on the horse-drawn tractor this afternoon," Levi said to Katie's back as she scrubbed her plate a little too hard. "Oh, and the parsnips, winter squash and beets all need tending."

Katie spun to face Levi. "And you need to be sure to balance the books at the end of the day and look over the figures for the last quarter and estimate sales for next quarter. That shouldn't be too hard, *ya*?"

"Not hard at all."

They stared each other down for a few beats before Gabriel said in a raised voice that carried from the living room, "I just finished the horse I was whittling for my little sister's Christmas present, so if you're finished bickering with your sweetheart, Levi, I'd like to get back to the farmwork."

Levi and Katie both jerked their attention to Gabriel, jaws slack like a pair of stunned fish. Gabriel dusted off his carving, blew on it to clear the last wood shavings and tucked it in his pocket as if he hadn't just said something outlandish. Levi and Katie remembered to close their mouths, then glanced at one another. She saw his cheeks were as red as hers felt. Levi quickly averted his gaze. "I…uh…best be getting back to the shop, ain't so?"

"What about your lunch?" Katie asked in a stammering voice.

"*Ach*, I'm not hungry," Levi said as he grabbed his hat from the peg by the door and crammed it on his head. "Just came by to check up on you, so…" He made a circular motion with his hand. "…carry on." And then he was gone.

Katie flinched. Levi could not have fled any faster. Was it because he was embarrassed and irritated that Gabriel would suggest such non-sense between Levi and her?

Or was it because Levi was actually sweet on her?

All his teasing, his good-natured but annoying debates, the smug half grin he kept on his face...

The sound of Gabriel chuckling from the next room interrupted Katie's revelation. The situation was so confusing she didn't know what to think. All she could do was shove her feet back into her waterproof outdoor boots, wrap herself in Levi's old barn coat and set out for the parsnip patch, leaving Gabriel and his ludicrous suggestion behind.

Levi could not concentrate for the rest of the day. He could not believe that Gabriel had said what he had. It wasn't good that Katie might think he was sweet on her. Not good at all.

The only thing worse was that he might actually *be* sweet on her.

The thought distracted him so much that he dropped a box of hand-painted glass Christmas ornaments. That added up to a total of $55.99 down the drain, including the cost of the cookie jar and gingerbread men. It also made Eliza scribble more notes on her yellow notepad.

Levi was thankful for the distraction when Simon came home from school, but he didn't stay in the shop for long. "Got to go check on Sugar Cookie and Fruit Cake," Simon shouted over his shoulder as he pounded up the stairs to their apartment.

Levi scratched his beard. "Has someone been baking?"

"Of course not, *Daed*. Sugar Cookie and Fruit Cake are my salamanders."

"Right. Send them my best, then."

"Sure will, *Daed*."

"And don't forget to do your chores."

"I won't."

Levi chuckled as his son disappeared up the staircase and the door banged shut. Simon really was one of a kind, just like Katie said.

Ach, there he went again, thinking of Katie. He would have to put her out of his mind. The best way to do that was to go over those figures she mentioned.

As it turned out, going over the accounting books was not as easy as Levi had thought it would be. By the end of the afternoon, he had accomplished little more than giving himself a headache. His vision was blurry and his back ached from hunching over the counter. Levi released a happy sigh when he finally looked up from the pages to see Eliza flipping the sign in the window from Open to Closed. The day was over and he could stop poring over those numbers. None of them made any sense to him. He was much better at fixing things with his hands than figuring sums. "See you later," Levi said as he slammed the black leather-bound book shut and rose from the wooden stool.

"*Ach*, I'm not leaving yet," Eliza said. "I have to see Katie first."

Levi sighed, but this time not so happily. "I'll go talk to her."

Eliza raised an eyebrow.

"I promise to tell her everything."

Eliza took her black coat from a peg on the wall, slid it on and pulled on a pair of black woolen mittens. "Then I will take you at your word, since I know how honest you are."

"Even when it makes me look bad?"

Eliza smiled. "Even then." She put her hand on the doorknob, hesitated and turned back toward Levi. "You did an okay job, you know."

"Just okay?" Levi asked with a grin.

"You did break over fifty dollars' worth of merchandise, so don't push it."

"Right."

"Maybe you're not cut out to work in a shop, but you tried and that's what counts, ain't so?"

"Thanks, Eliza. That means a lot, coming from you."

Eliza looked pleased as she adjusted a woolen mitten.

"Say hello to Priss for me."

"I will. She still talks about that hayride you took her and Simon on last month."

Levi remembered that afternoon with a smile. Simon had been a little chatterbox, pointing out all the amphibian habitats they passed. It seemed like ages ago—before Katie had burst into his life like a... He wasn't sure how to finish that sentence. A few weeks ago he would have said like a wildcat, ready to fight. But now it felt more as though she had burst into his life like a breath of fresh air. Why on earth he felt that way, he didn't know. All they did was disagree over every little thing.

Or did they just offer one another a fresh perspective?

Levi liked that Katie didn't back down. He liked that she pushed him, challenged him to be his best self. He liked that she wasn't intimidated. If anything, she was the one who was intimidating, with that fierce glint in her eye and her mouth set in a tight line while she raised her chin and stared him down. The image made him feel oddly warm inside, as though he had just drunk a mug of hot chocolate.

"She's hoping for another one at Christmas," Eliza said, her hand still on the doorknob.

"Another what?" Levi pulled himself back from the image of Katie in his head.

"Another hayride."

"Oh, right. *Ya*, I don't see why not, weather permitting."

"*Danki*. She'll be happy to hear that." Eliza slipped out the door, and Levi followed not far behind. He might as well get the conversation with Katie over with. He was going to have to admit that he wasn't quite the shopkeeper he had boasted of. Well, didn't the Scriptures say pride cometh before destruction and a haughty spirit cometh before a fall? He had walked right into that one, really, and gotten exactly what he deserved.

Levi found Katie hunched over an assortment of metal parts spread across a green tarp on the concrete floor of the barn. He hovered in the doorway, watching her pick up a metal gear, turn it over in her hand, then set it down again. The late-afternoon sun shone across the barn in rays that highlighted the soft curve of her cheek and jaw. She selected a screw from a pile on the tarp, held it up, squinted at it for a moment, then tossed it down again and sighed.

Levi cleared his throat. Katie stiffened and looked up. "I didn't see you there."

He smiled. "Too busy being an engineer, ain't so?"

Katie didn't smile in return. "I, uh…" She

puffed out her cheeks and exhaled. "I'm afraid I've ruined your tractor. I tried to follow the instructions from the manufacturer." She picked up a sheet of paper and waved it in the air. "But it's hopeless, Levi. Absolutely hopeless." She squeezed her eyes shut and shook her head. "I'm sorry. I don't think it can be fixed after what I've done to it."

"Is that so?" Levi asked mildly.

"For sure and certain."

Levi walked across the barn to where she sat slumped over the mechanical parts. "Looks like you managed to take the whole thing apart."

"And now I can't put it back together again. I was just trying to fix the broken gear, and next thing I knew…" She swept a hand over the dismantled parts strewn across the tarp. "…this happened."

Levi lowered himself to sit on the tarp beside her. She kept her eyes down and her lips tight.

"It's not so bad," Levi said.

"I shouldn't have tried. I should have known I was getting in over my head. Gabriel left to mend the fence—I couldn't do that, either, and he had to go back and finish the job for me after lunch. He said Old Gus might get out otherwise. So, instead of doing something reasonable, like feeding and watering the livestock or oiling harnesses, I took this on."

Levi looked over at her and chuckled. She glanced up and frowned. "I wish you wouldn't laugh at me. I'm at a pretty low point right now. I guess I'm not so *gut* at admitting I didn't live up to my boasting." She looked at the mechanical parts in front of her. "But I can't hide my failure from you."

"I'm not laughing at you," Levi said. "Well, not exactly. I'm laughing at both of us."

Katie creased her brow and moved her gaze back to him. "What do you mean?"

"Let's just say you're not the only one who failed to live up to your boasts today."

"You mean…" A faint smile appeared on Katie's lips.

"Yup. I pretty much crashed and burned at the shop after all my big talk. Turns out keeping a shop isn't so simple after all."

Katie straightened up and her smile widened. "What happened?"

"First of all, I broke a cookie jar. And a box of glass Christmas ornaments. Then I took forever trying to find an item for a customer—"

"We had a customer?"

"*Ya.* But she left without buying anything. Which is kind of my point."

"Right," Katie said. "Go on."

"She wanted a very specific porcelain figurine of a windmill that says—"

"We don't have it."

"You know that for a fact, just like that?"

Katie shrugged and looked sheepish. "It's my job to know."

"And you're better at it than I am," Levi said. "There's so much stuff in that place I don't know how you keep it all straight. Anyway, I couldn't find it and her daughter got tired of waiting and that was that."

"That's why I keep a basket of cookies on the counter. Children who come into the shop get one for free."

"*Ach, gut* idea. I wish I'd thought of that."

"I should have told you."

"I wouldn't have listened."

"Probably not," Katie said.

They both laughed.

"Did you show her the other porcelain figurines?" Katie asked after a moment. "We have some similar ones. There's one of a red barn. And another of a little cottage with a wheelbarrow in the yard. And we have a porcelain buggy and—" Levi shook his head, and Katie cut her sentence short. "And I guess you didn't offer to try and find it from the wholesaler and special order it for her?"

"Uh, no." Levi took off his hat and ran his hand through his hair. "And I couldn't make heads or tails of all those numbers in the ledgers. Like I said, I'm not very *gut* at running a shop, apparently."

He expected Katie to give him a hard time for losing business, but instead she gave him an encouraging smile. "And I'm not very good at farmwork. So I guess that makes us even."

"Guess so," Levi said. "I did get that customer's card, though, so maybe you can find the figurine and contact her."

Katie's expression brightened. "*Gut* work, Levi!"

"*Ach*, she offered it. I didn't think to ask."

Katie laughed. "At least you're honest."

"I am. And there's something else I haven't told you yet."

Katie's laughter trailed off and she frowned. "What?"

"That I know all there is to know about dismantling and reassembling mechanical farm equipment."

"Really?"

"Sure. I'll have this back together in no time."

"How...?"

"It's my job to know," Levi said with a sheepish grin.

Katie's eyes lit up. "You mean I haven't ruined your tractor?"

"Nah. I can get it put back together, no problem." He elbowed her side. "And this time I'm not boasting. It's just something I know how to do. No big deal."

"It's a big deal to me," Katie said. "I couldn't put this thing back together to save my life."

"Then it's a *gut* thing your life doesn't depend on it."

"So you know what this thing actually does?" Katie asked as she picked up a metal gear.

"Ya." Levi reached for it, and his fingers brushed hers as she handed it over. Her skin felt warm and soft against his. Their hands lingered for just a moment. Then she jerked hers away and averted her gaze. Levi felt so flustered that he fumbled with the gear and dropped it. He glanced over and saw that Katie's cheeks were flushed. Something was happening between them.

And he couldn't help but like it.

Bishop Amos stopped by the farm after supper to see how their day had gone.

"Just in time for dessert," Levi said as he opened the door and ushered Amos to the kitchen table.

Amos chuckled and patted his midsection. "My belly keeps *gut* time."

"We've got cookies!" Simon shouted before stuffing a big one into his mouth.

"Willkumm," Katie said as she got up to grab another plate.

"Well, you two seem to be in *gut* spirits," Amos said with a knowing look as he settled into a chair. "Looks like my plan worked, *ya*?"

Katie and Levi glanced at one another and smiled. *"Ya,"* they both admitted.

"I was terrible at running the shop," Levi said.

"And I definitely underestimated how hard Levi has to work," Katie said as she set a plate in front of Amos, then sat down. "Every time I got something checked off the list, there was something else waiting for me."

Levi nodded his head and passed the tin of oatmeal cookies to Amos.

Katie turned to Levi. "You have so many different crops, plus the dairy cows. Why not just focus on one or two things? Wouldn't that be simpler?"

"Not a lot of land to go around in Lancaster County, so our farms are pretty small. You have to make the most of every acre and keep producing year-round. So we have winter wheat in the ground now, plus the parsnips, winter squash and beets, which will go through December. That keeps us selling into the cold weather. The small herd of dairy cows supplements our income by producing throughout the winter—not to mention the rest of the year—and then there's the corn and other feed crops in the spring and summer. Cobbled all together, it gets us by. It's the way most of the Amish farms do things around here."

"Do you ever think about doing something else?" Katie asked, then flinched and shook her head. "I didn't mean—I'm not suggesting you give the land to me. I just wondered..."

"Why I'm so set on this work?"

"*Ya.* I hear the majority of Amish in Lancaster County don't farm."

Everyone's attention was on Levi, but he didn't respond. Katie wondered if she had said the wrong thing.

Simon reached for a second cookie while Amos quietly chewed a bite of his. Katie's eyes stayed on Levi. "What is it?" she asked.

Levi cleared his throat. "*Ach*, nothing." He glanced at Simon. "Just that, well, this place means a lot to me. It's not just about owning farmland in Lancaster County. It's...something more."

Katie leaned forward. Gone was the joking, smirking Levi. This man was serious, thoughtful. And she sensed a flicker of pain behind his eyes.

"We moved here right after Simon's mother died. We lost her in childbirth."

"I'm so sorry," Katie said.

Levi picked at the cookie in his hand. "Sometimes *Gott*'s will isn't easy."

Katie didn't know what to say to that, so she just nodded.

"I was looking for a fresh start and took the job with Fannie. She became like family. Simon grew up here. I've poured everything into this place. It's our home and our sanctuary."

"I can't imagine how hard it must have been…"

Levi glanced at Simon. "He knows how much his *mamm* loved him, even though she didn't get to raise him. I've tried to do my best…" Levi put down his cookie, then picked it up again.

"Rachel was a *gut* woman," Amos said quietly.

"*Mamm*'s why I love zoology," Simon piped up. "She was real *gut* at that kind of stuff, right, *Daed*?"

"For sure and certain, *sohn*." Levi looked at Simon with glistening eyes. Then he cleared his throat and said, "How'd you get on with the cows today, Katie? No problems after I left this morning?"

Katie felt a twinge of guilt when she remembered how she had accused Levi of trying to steal an old lady's money. It was clear he had good reason to want to stay on the land. She debated for a moment whether or not to say something—perhaps even apologize—but it was obvious Levi wanted to change the subject. "We got on just fine. Are cows really that dangerous?"

"June's not. She's an old sweetheart."

"You mean you were just trying to scare me?"

Levi shrugged and flashed a sheepish grin. "Not exactly. You can never be too careful around livestock. Statistically, they do cause a lot of farm injuries."

"I'm not asking about statistics."

"Okay, okay. All my cows are gentle. You have to be mindful around them, like with all livestock, but mine aren't really that dangerous. Otherwise I would never have let you milk them." He paused and stared into her eyes with a serious expression, then continued in a low, determined voice, "I would never put you in danger."

As they stared into one another's eyes, Katie could feel her cheeks flush and her mouth go dry.

Amos pushed back his chair, jolting Katie back to the present. "Glad to see you're getting along better," he said and stood up. "I'll check in again soon. Christmas is only a few weeks away."

For the first time, those words did not feel threatening. Katie was beginning to believe she and Levi could find a way to make this work… together.

Chapter Eight

After doing the morning milking, Levi doubled back to his apartment to get Simon off to school, whistling as he walked through the frosty morning. The rising sun shimmered across the farmyard and highlighted the white crystals coating the grass. Everything felt a little brighter, a little lighter after his time with Katie yesterday. She had been open, honest and understanding. She had been…

Lovely.

He felt a jolt of excitement that he might see her as he cut through the shop. But it was still too early. The Christmas candles were unlit, the space dark and silent. He began creating scenarios in his head for an excuse to drop into the shop later in hopes of seeing her. *Ach*, he was being *narrisch*. It was crazy to indulge in these emotions. He and Katie had managed to become friends, but that didn't mean it was a good idea to take things any further.

Even if he *was* whistling and taking the steps to the apartment two at a time at the thought of seeing her again.

Levi found Simon still in bed, head crammed underneath the pillow, his battery-powered alarm clock turned off. "Best get a move on," Levi said and pulled the pillow away. Simon yawned and rubbed his eyes. His hair stuck up like a rooster's comb.

"Slept through your alarm?" Levi asked.

"*Ya.* I was up late reading about the life cycle of the eastern newt. Fascinating stuff, *Daed.*"

"Is that right?" Levi tousled his son's hair and made a mental note to make sure Simon turned off his lamp on time tonight.

There was a knock on the door, which was unusual. Levi's stomach did a little flip-flop at the thought that it might be Katie. "Better hurry up so you're not late again," Levi said and left Simon to get dressed while he answered the door.

He was thrilled to see it *was* her. Rubbing the back of his neck, he felt suddenly nervous. "It's great to see you." Had she come up just to say hello? The thought made him feel all weak inside.

But Katie didn't return his welcoming grin. "We have to talk."

"Oh. Okay. Now?"

"*Ya.*"

"Is everything *oll recht*?"

Katie looked down at a paper in her hand and bit her lip.

Levi stepped back and waved her inside. "*Kumme*, sit." His mood deflated as he ushered her to the cushioned rocking chair. He took the less comfortable straight-backed wooden chair.

"It's bad news, Levi."

"I gathered that. Best just get it over with."

Katie nodded. "*Aenti* Fannie took out a second mortgage to make up for the loss in business revenue. A letter from the bank just came. Seems that she fell behind in the mortgage payments. Way behind. We're…" Katie's voice caught in her throat. She swallowed hard and handed him the paper. "We're in real danger of losing this place."

Levi scanned the paper, his heart throbbing in his ears. He felt time stand still as he read the words, reread them and then reread them once again. This could not be happening. It simply could not be happening. He shook his head and stared at the paper, unable to respond.

"Did you know about this?"

Levi's head jerked up. "No. Of course not. I would have said something. I would have *done* something."

Katie's mouth was set in a tight line. He couldn't

tell if she believed him. Her expression made him doubt himself. Was there something more he could have done? "Katie. Say something."

"I don't know what to say. How could this have happened? How could you have lived here and let it happen? You knew *Aenti* Fannie wasn't able to keep up with everything anymore."

"I was never in charge of the books. That wasn't my job."

Katie gave him a level stare that made him feel like a stranger. "Maybe you should have made it your job."

Levi crumpled the paper in his hand. "Maybe *you* should have been here to do it," he said.

"You know why I wasn't here," Katie said. "You're not being fair."

"*I'm* not being fair? After everything—" He cut his eyes toward Simon's bedroom and lowered his voice. "After everything I did for Fannie, you're going to blame me for this?"

"I—I—don't know what to think…" Katie stood up abruptly. "We can't… I can't…" She shook her head, hesitated, then turned on her heels and stormed to the door.

Levi stood up. "Katie."

She didn't answer or turn around. Instead, she fled down the stairs, the sound of her footsteps drifting back through the shocked silence in the room.

* * *

Katie had a headache. Of course she did. She had been clenching her jaw ever since she read that terrible letter from the bank. And then she had gone and made everything worse by blaming Levi. That had been unfair. But it made her feel better to have someone to blame. She felt that she had more control over the situation that way.

It was too scary to think there was no one to blame, no way to control the outcome.

She closed her eyes, took a deep breath and exhaled.

Footsteps padded across the shop. "Are you all right?"

Katie opened her eyes to see Eliza peering at her over the rims of her oversized glasses.

Katie forced a smile and straightened up. "*Ya.* Of course." Katie didn't want to worry Eliza, especially this close to Christmas. She also hated to admit that life was spinning out beyond her control. She had forged an identity of self-reliance while caring for her family and hated to feel helpless.

Eliza studied Katie for a moment. "You don't look all right."

Katie frowned and smoothed the front of her apron. "Just a lot to do… A lot to figure out…"

Eliza hesitated then and said, "We can cancel Thanksgiving. If it's too much for you."

"What?"

Eliza stared at Katie as if it were obvious. "Thanksgiving. We all have Thanksgiving here every year." Eliza's expression suddenly shifted. Her eyes widened. "Oh. You weren't planning to…" Eliza's cheeks reddened, and she looked down at her clasped hands. "I didn't mean to imply… It's just that…"

Katie had forgotten all about Thanksgiving. Her eyes shot to the calendar on the wall. Thanksgiving was tomorrow? Impossible. She had been so caught up in running the business that she had forgotten what really mattered, like giving thanks to *Gott* and connecting with the people around her. "Of course we'll have Thanksgiving here! It will be great." Her mind began to race a mile a minute as she tried to figure out how to make time for all the preparations.

Eliza's face brightened with a relieved smile. "*Mamm*'s been looking forward to it for weeks. And Priss, too, of course.

"*Wunderbaar.*" Katie paused, then asked, "How many should I expect?"

"Just Priss, *Mamm*, Gabriel and his *aenti* Mary, Levi and Simon, Sadie and her six siblings, their parents, and me. And whoever else shows up. You know how it is—Fannie's doors were always open."

Katie felt overwhelmed just thinking about it. She wanted to be a welcoming place for everyone to gather, but there was no time left to prepare. Not to mention the fact that Levi would be sitting across the table from her. The thought of seeing him again after this morning's conversation twisted her stomach into knots.

"*Mamm* and I will be here tomorrow morning to help you cook," Eliza said. "Five a.m. sharp."

"I suppose I ought to close the shop on Thanksgiving... I just thought some early Black Friday customers might come in."

"*Ach*, Fannie never worried about that. She always said celebrating our blessings came first." Eliza frowned at Katie. "And besides, it doesn't seem right to work on Thanksgiving. You should be with family that day."

"I don't have any family here," Katie murmured. In fact, she barely had any friends here. Just Levi—and that relationship felt strained and tentative. She had barely gone out since she moved to Bluebird Hills, putting all her time and energy into the shop instead. She had become isolated in her small world, completely distracted by her failing business.

Eliza squinted through her glasses. "You have us."

The words hit Katie harder than she expected. Eliza was an employee—and a difficult one, at that. Did she really see Katie as more than a boss? How much had Katie failed to notice about the people around her? How much had she pushed them away without even realizing it?

Katie woke before the rooster crowed the next morning—Thanksgiving morning—and quickly slipped into her best-for-church purple cape dress, apron and *kapp* and padded downstairs. She both dreaded and hoped to see Levi in the kitchen. Her emotions warred within her. She missed his teasing. She missed the way he made her laugh and the way he smelled like leather and pine when he came inside for the evening. That realization made her stomach jump in alarm.

But, even though she missed him, the thought of speaking to him made her insides churn. Did he really think she had abandoned *Aenti* Fannie without a care? *Could* he have done more to prevent *Aenti* Fannie from getting so behind on the mortgage?

The kitchen was cold and bare when Katie entered it. Her feet echoed in the silence as she walked to the woodstove. She opened the metal door, added a log from the woodpile and shut the door with a gentle bang. A warm orange glow shimmered behind the metal grate and warmed her skin through her thin purple dress.

She sighed and looked around the still, quiet room. Nothing felt right without Levi's mocking smile or playful jokes.

She frowned at that. This was not part of the plan. She had come to take back her property and make a new life for herself—not develop a connection with the man who had fought her every step of the way.

But had he really fought her? Or had he just done what he thought was best? Hadn't he been willing to compromise with her ever since she arrived?

And her response was to accuse him of failing *Aenti* Fannie.

Katie trudged to the cabinets, where she pulled out the ingredients to whip up a quick batch of muffins for Eliza and her *mamm*, who would be arriving soon.

Katie's eyes wandered as she stirred the batter in the big wooden mixing bowl. She found herself searching for a glimpse of Levi in the farmyard beyond the kitchen window. She scanned the sprawling white barn and outbuildings, the fenced enclosure where Old Gus stood in the frost, his sleek black mane rippling in the breeze as the faint glow of moonlight silhouetted his massive bulk. He snorted at the chickens that pecked the frozen ground near his massive hooves. Katie gazed across the bare, brown fields that lay beyond the barn. The glow of Levi's lantern in the early-morning darkness was nowhere in sight.

If she did see him, would she apologize? She wasn't sure what she would say. It was all so awkward. She knew she was at fault—but so was he. She stirred the batter harder. A big, fat drop flew from the bowl and splattered across her apron. Katie dropped the spoon and sighed. She had to fix the rift between her and Levi, but she didn't want to admit she was wrong.

She whispered a quick prayer to *Gott* for help overcoming her pride, then braced herself for a difficult but necessary conversation. Maybe they could even find a way to work together. Katie shook her head at the thought that Bishop Amos might have known what he was doing all along.

Katie wiped her hands on a dish towel and began to untie her apron. But then there was a quick knock on the door, and it opened with a blast of cold air. Eliza, Lovina and Priss breezed in, chattering and smiling. She had missed her chance.

Lovina strolled into the kitchen holding a brown paper grocery bag. It was clear she was used to letting herself in. "Happy Thanksgiving! Ready to get started?"

Katie blinked a few times as Lovina strode

across the room, riffled through a couple of drawers until she found an apron, tied it around her waist, then began rummaging through the cabinets.

"Don't mind me," Lovina said as she set a tub of shortening on the counter with a thud. "Fannie and I went way back. I know my way around this kitchen."

"Ya," Katie said. "I can see that."

Eliza pulled a stack of recipe cards from her pocket and began flipping through them. Both women wore the same big glasses, had the same bony elbows and maintained the same no-nonsense expression.

Simon padded into the room with his hair sticking straight up. He rubbed his eyes as his mouth cracked open in an enormous yawn. "I love Thanksgiving, but why does it have to start so early?" Then his attention shot to Priss, and he perked up. "Oh, hey, Priss! Want to go outside and pet Old Gus?"

"Ya." Priss flashed a shy but genuine smile.

"Don't wander off," Eliza warned as she adjusted Priss's warm winter kerchief over her *kapp* and retied it beneath her chin. Simon threw on his coat and pushed his feet into a pair of rubber boots. "And keep your mittens on!" Eliza added as the two *kinner* scampered out the door, letting it slam behind them. "It's cold out there," Eliza added, too late for them to hear.

"Levi not around today?" Lovina asked without turning around from the counter.

"He's outside, I guess," Katie said.

"Hmm," Lovina murmured. "That's not like him. He usually sticks around for breakfast with us when we come to cook Thanksgiving dinner. Have to chase him away most years. He's always trying to sneak a few bites of food before it's ready."

Katie looked down. "Well, I guess he's just busy today." *Busy avoiding me.*

"He'll show up sooner or later," Lovina said as she squinted at a measuring spoon, then exchanged it for a smaller one.

Not this year, Katie thought with a pang of regret. She had made sure of that.

Levi's attention kept wandering toward the kitchen window as he took care of the farm chores that had to be done whether or not it was a holiday. He could make out a blur of movement from behind the glass panes as laughter drifted through the still November air. When he walked closer, he caught a savory whiff of brown gravy, roasting meat and baking bread. This was the first year he hadn't popped into the kitchen to joke with the women and steal bites of food fresh from the oven. He shivered and turned up the collar of his barn coat. What was Katie doing right now? He could imagine her darting from the counter to the propane-powered refrigerator, forehead creased in concentration as she followed a recipe from the handwritten book she kept beside the big blue cookie jar. Funny how she had slid into his life and rearranged his kitchen and somehow the changes felt right, like she—and her kitchen accessories—had always been there.

Well, it *had* felt right. Now he didn't know what to feel. He hadn't spoken to her since their conversation about the mortgage. How could he face her after she'd blamed him for the debts the business faced?

It was bad enough that he blamed himself.

He kept going over the past several years in his mind, second-guessing himself, wondering what more he could have done to prevent Fannie from taking out that mortgage without telling him. After everything that he had put into the farm, he had still failed somehow. And now Simon would face the consequences. His chest felt heavy at the thought of telling the boy. How could he take his son away from the only home he had ever known? The home Levi had created to keep them safe from pain and loss?

Soon, it would all be gone, leaving only memories behind.

It seemed to Levi that everything he touched turned to dust, to be swept away and lost forever. First his wife, now his land and livelihood. Where would he and Simon go? What would they do?

He shook his head and turned away from the kitchen window, back toward the barn. How could he have let himself develop feelings for Katie? She would never want a man like him, a man who let an entire farm slip through his fingers.

Levi heard a shout followed by a carefree giggle. Then Simon and Priss zipped around the corner of the barn, raced past him and disappeared behind the grain bin. Katie already refused to speak to him because he had lost the business. Would Simon lose respect for him, too?

It seemed only a matter of time before the entire community saw his failures and held him accountable.

Levi kept himself busy in the barn long after the necessary farm chores were finished, just so he could avoid Katie. He heard the crunch of gravel as buggies arrived with visitors carrying warm casserole dishes and baskets of fresh-baked yeast rolls. Their friendly greetings drifted through the cracks in the barn walls along with the cold. He rubbed his hands to warm them and headed outside to make sure the entrance to the grain bin was locked. The farm was full of dangers for careless *kinner*.

The kitchen door swung open as he trudged across the farmyard, and Lovina's small figure appeared in the threshold. "Everyone inside!" she hollered in a voice that was too big for her petite frame. "Food's getting cold!" The *kinner* dashed past Levi—seemingly from out of nowhere—scampered up the back porch steps and bustled into the kitchen with sparkling eyes and cheeks bright from the cold.

Levi followed. He would do his best to act normal, even though his world was slipping away from him. He left his muddy boots on the porch and walked into a house filled with warmth and delicious smells. The kitchen swarmed with people, but it didn't feel crowded. Instead, the bustling scene felt cozy and familiar. Except Fannie was missing. Her absence left a gap in his heart—a gap that Katie had somehow filled without his even realizing it.

Funny how you don't notice how gut *something is until you don't have it anymore*, he thought. They had begun to have *something* together—back when they thought they would keep their home and livelihood. Now he couldn't see how they had any shot for a future together. He could barely imagine what the future held for him and Simon, much less for him and anyone else. Had it only been since yesterday morning that reality struck? It felt like an eternity.

His eyes cut to Katie. She glanced up at him, and her expression hardened before she quickly turned. So that was how it would be. Well, he could keep ignoring her, too, since that was clearly what she wanted. He just had to push down the hurt and force a smile for company.

"And where have you been?" Lovina asked, stepping in front of him with her hands on her hips. She had to crane her neck back to meet his eyes but still managed to seem intimidating.

Levi rubbed the back of his neck. "Uh, you know, farm chores and stuff…"

"Humph. Doesn't take half the day to feed and water the stock. *Gott* gave us plenty of days for working, but today is a day for visiting and giving thanks. Now come here." Lovina motioned with her hands, then pulled him into a hug when he stepped forward. "Haven't seen you enough lately." She let go of him and eased back to study his expression. "Everything *oll recht*?"

"*Ya,*" Levi said. "*Ya,* of course."

Lovina narrowed her eyes. "You sure about that? I can read your face like a book, you know."

"*Ach*, I'm fine." Levi waved his hand dismissively. "Time to eat, ain't so?"

"*Ya*. Time to eat." But her eyes lingered on him for a few beats, and Levi knew she didn't believe he was fine.

A hearty slap on the back jolted Levi. He turned to see Gabriel's teasing grin. "Trying to make me look lazy, huh?"

"Just had some extra work to do, that's all."

"It's not like you to miss out on food. I've snuck half a pie already." Gabriel patted his stomach, then nodded toward Katie, who stood across the room with her back to them. "You're not the only one acting funny, you know. Something's going on with you two, ain't so?"

Levi's eyebrows slammed down. "*Nee,*" he whispered harshly. "There is nothing—absolutely nothing—going on between us."

Gabriel lifted his hands in a gesture of surrender. "Whoa, okay. Looks like I touched a nerve."

"I'm just hungry," Levi said. "Low blood sugar."

Lovina and Gabriel exchanged a quick glance. "Okay," Gabriel said. "If you say so."

Levi sighed and headed to the table. This was going to be a very long meal.

Katie's heart did a little flip-flop when she saw Levi come into the kitchen. Had he always been that tall and handsome? Yes, he had. But he had not always worn that stern frown. She was used to seeing a warm smile that crinkled the corners of his eyes and brightened his entire face.

He refused to look at her as everyone shuffled into their seats at the main table and at the folding tables set up for the occasion, then said a silent prayer of thanks. Katie sat directly across from Levi at the head of the main table—or the foot, depending on whom you asked—so it was not easy for him to avoid her eyes. But he managed. He never glanced up at her as he carved the turkey or when he passed dishes of food. Katie felt a lump in her stomach as she realized how easy it seemed for him to ignore her. Did he feel nothing for her?

Well, he probably did feel something—just not the emotions she *wanted* him to feel for her.

Katie refused to look at him, since he refused to look at her. Instead, she chatted with the people seated beside her. Gabriel's aunt Mary was in her early thirties, much younger than Katie had expected, and they got along wonderfully. Sadie's father seemed somewhat stern, but he answered Katie's questions politely before turning to discuss this year's crop of winter wheat with Gabriel. Sadie, who was seated farther down the table, stuck out from among her younger sisters. She seemed to radiate energy and charisma, while they all appeared shy and unassertive. At one point during the meal, Sadie told a particularly funny story that made Gabriel guffaw. Even Levi chuckled—his first hint of amusement he'd showed the entire meal. But Sadie's father shot her a disapproving look. Sadie looked down and did not tell another joke for the rest of the meal.

Katie could see that Sadie needed an outlet to express herself. She seemed so full of life and energy. Katie remembered that Sadie wanted to sell her artwork and wondered if she had done the right thing to dismiss the idea. Katie pushed a serving of green beans around her plate with her fork as she pondered the situation. No, she thought after a moment, it wasn't her job to give Sadie an outlet. Besides, what would Eliza and the rest of the church district think? She should leave well enough alone and keep things the way they had always been.

Except the way things had always been was no longer working—and apparently it hadn't been working for some time. If Aunt Fannie's ways worked, they wouldn't be drowning in debt right now.

"You look too serious for the dinner table," Lovina said.

Katie looked up from her plate. "*Ach*, well,

I was just thinking about the shop. I have a lot to do…"

"Not today, you don't," Lovina said. "Enjoy your blessings." She motioned to Katie's half-eaten plate of food. "And eat up."

Katie glanced around the table at the smiling, glowing faces. Silverware clinked and wooden serving spoons thumped against serving bowls. The room radiated warmth and love. But Katie had been too busy worrying about the future to notice. There were still plenty of blessings to count, despite what she was going through with the business. She counted sixteen blessings right here—each of the people sitting around her table and the folding tables set up alongside it. She offered a quick prayer of thanks to *Gott* for these people who had gone from strangers to friends in the blink of an eye.

Katie's eyes moved to Levi. He must have felt her watching him, because his eyes jerked up and stared back at her. Her breath caught in her throat at the intensity of his gaze. Despite everything, it felt so good to see him opposite her at the table. *Their* table.

And in that moment, she knew he was the blessing in her life that she had taken most for granted.

Chapter Nine

The morning after Thanksgiving, Levi heard the sound of boots slogging through the mud and was surprised to see Katie striding toward him with a basket in her hands and a grim look on her face. He set down his mallet and watched her approach. "Didn't expect to see you today," he said once she was in earshot. After all, she had ignored him throughout Thanksgiving, even though they had been sitting at the same table.

Katie looked down. "No, I guess not."

Levi stared at her, waiting and wondering what she wanted. Hopefully not to bring up his failure again. Normally criticism rolled off his back. He preferred to see the humor in a situation rather than the problem. But something about Katie Schwartz made him want to impress her. He had not felt that way since...

Rachel.

Levi frowned and shifted his weight from one leg to the other. Katie was nothing like Rachel. She could never be like Rachel. She was willful, argumentative, quick to blame... He hardened his expression and waited for the verbal blow she was sure to give him.

"I...um... I came to apologize," Katie said. "And bring a peace offering."

Levi felt a weight lift from his chest.

She held up the basket. "The way to a man's heart is through his stomach, *ya*?" Her face instantly turned pink. "I didn't mean, that is, I'm not trying to— I didn't mean to suggest..."

Levi gave her a smile. He would forgive her, of course. In fact, he already had. But that didn't mean he was going to let her off easily.

"You didn't mean to suggest that you're trying to win my heart?"

Katie sucked her breath in between her teeth. "*Nee*, it's just an expression."

"An expression about winning a man's heart."

"*Ya*. I mean, *nee*. I mean..." She cleared her throat and shoved the basket toward him. "Let's eat."

Levi chuckled and took the basket.

"I just meant the way to a man's heart *as a friend seeking forgiveness* is through his stomach," Katie added, her face still pink.

"Ah. I see." He grinned at her. "So I'm your friend now, huh?"

"Well…" She swallowed, looked down at her hands and adjusted her brown woolen mittens. "I guess. If you still want to be my friend after I blamed you for the farm's financial situation. That was wrong of me."

"It's okay," Levi said and looked into her eyes. "I understand." His gaze bored into hers.

"You do?" Katie asked, her face open and trusting.

He dropped his eyes. "*Ya*. Because it *is* my fault. You were only telling the truth."

"What? No!" Katie shook her head, eyes wide. "I was wrong. I only blamed you because I panicked. It made me feel better to blame you, because if it was your fault, then maybe you could fix it." She sighed and looked away. "And I guess it felt better to blame you than to blame myself. I wasn't here. You were. I'm more at fault than you. At least you tried." A single tear slipped from her eye and trailed down her cheek.

"Oh, Katie." Levi gently wiped the tear with his finger. Katie's gaze flicked to him in surprise. Levi hoped he hadn't overstepped. He backed away from her and murmured, "I, um…" He could see how vulnerable she was beneath her tough exterior. He wanted to scoop her into his arms and hold her until she never felt the need to cry again. He forced himself to keep his hands by his sides. "I'm sorry I've made you feel that way. It isn't your fault. None of it is. We can't always understand *Gott*'s plans for us, but we can always trust them. We have to trust that He kept you at home with your *mamm* for a reason."

Katie managed a crooked smile. Her eyes were still moist with tears. "Only if you can trust that He allowed the property to fall into debt for a reason and that there was nothing more you could have done, even though you were here. My *mamm* always says, 'Do your best and let *Gott* do the rest.' And I'm certain sure you did your best."

Levi thought about that for a moment, his gaze still locked on Katie's hazel eyes. He nodded and felt a release from deep within. "*Ya.* I did my best."

"Well, then that's all anyone can ask of you."

Levi grinned. "Goes for you, too, you know."

"Okay, so we both stop blaming ourselves."

"*Ya,*" Levi said. "That's exactly what we do." He held her eyes, and emotion rippled between them, then settled inside him like a warm light. He didn't know how to handle that feeling. He and Katie had finally become friends. If they tried to take things further, it could throw everything off track. Not to mention that if they lost the farm, she would probably go home to Indiana. He would have no home to offer her and no way to support her, at least not for a while. So he dropped his eyes to the picnic basket and whipped off the red-and-white-checkered cloth to reveal two olive green thermoses and two thick slabs of buttered homemade bread.

"Chicken noodle soup," Katie said. "Seemed right for the weather."

"You do realize it's too cold for a picnic, *ya*?" Levi kept his tone light.

Katie offered a shaky smile. "*Ya*, but I had to do something nice, ain't so?"

Levi picked up one of the thermoses and set the basket on a grassy patch of ground. "Hot lunch is much appreciated." He unscrewed the lid and blew over the top of the broth. "Sure smells *gut*."

Katie laughed. "I'm glad, but I have to confess it's from a can. I didn't have time to cook from scratch."

Levi took a sip, swallowed and nodded. "Warms the bones just the same."

Katie watched Levi take another sip from the green thermos. "So, are we okay, then?"

"*Ya*. We're okay." Levi bent down and plucked the remaining thermos from the basket. "Have lunch with me."

"Danki."

"Don't thank me," Levi said with a twinkle in his eye. "You're the one who brought it."

"You know what I mean." Katie hesitated. "Right?"

"Ya. I know what you mean," Levi said gently.

Katie nodded, unscrewed the lid of her thermos and took a cautious sip. She flinched and jerked her mouth away.

"Too hot?"

"Ya." Katie left the lid off so the soup could cool. Steam curled into the air and warmed her face. "We don't know what *Gott*'s will is in all this. Until we do, we have to keep doing our best to save the property."

Levi gave a thoughtful nod as he swallowed his soup. "I was planning on getting started on that list I came up with when Bishop Amos was here. Haven't gotten to it yet, what with Thanksgiving and all." Levi studied the thermos in his hands. "I hope you're not still against my making those changes."

Katie shook her head. "No. I just…it's just hard because I don't want anything to change around here."

Levi responded, "Whatever we've been doing isn't working, so we have to change things. Lots of things, probably—a lot more than what's on that list." Glancing up, he gave Katie a reassuring look. "Although you've already gotten a *gut* start, you know."

Katie looked perplexed.

"Eliza's doing much better with customers."

Katie laughed. "Ah, yes. We've been working on changing how she talks to people."

Levi lifted his eyebrows. "See, was that so hard?"

Katie laughed again. "Actually, it was. Eliza is not the easiest student. But that's not what I meant. I was talking about the stock, the look of the shop—that kind of stuff. *Aenti* Fannie never changed a thing. People like that. They shop at my—at our—store because it's familiar, comforting, traditional."

"True." Levi propped an elbow on the top slat of the fence and leaned against it. "But it's also run-down and uninteresting."

Katie's attention shot from her thermos to Levi. "Run-down and uninteresting? How can you say that?"

"Because it's true."

Katie's brow crinkled. "The shop is charmingly rustic and cozily predictable. People like that. People *need* that."

"It's been neglected for years. Just wait until I fix it up. You'll be pleasantly surprised."

"I hope you're right, Levi Miller."

Levi flashed a boyish grin. "I'm always right, Katie Schwartz."

Katie shook her head in playful irritation, then quickly sobered. "And what about the farm? Do you have plans to change everything here too?" She swept a hand across the rolling brown hills and yellow fields.

"Not everything."

Katie frowned. Her finger tapped against the thermos. "Like what?"

"Oh, I don't know. I haven't figured that out. If I had any great ideas, I would have followed through with them by now."

"Well, I was thinking, maybe I could take a look at the farm's accounting books," Katie said. "I'm pretty *gut* with numbers. I don't mean to sound prideful. It's just something that's always come easily to me. Maybe I can find a way to save some overhead."

"It think that would be great," Levi said.

"So, we're..." Katie looked up at Levi with questioning eyes. "We're in this together now?"

Levi stared back into her eyes and answered with a firm but gentle voice. "*Ya.* We're in this together. All the way."

Katie swallowed hard. "Then we better tell Bishop Amos the competition he put in place the day I arrived to decide who gets to manage the property is over." She hesitated. "If that's what you meant."

"Ya," Levi said. "It's definitely over."

Amos and Edna were pleased but not surprised to hear that Katie and Levi wanted to stop competing for control and manage the property as a team. "Fannie was no fool," Edna said with a chuckle. "She would never have made such a *narrisch* plan if she didn't think you two could work together."

"That's for certain sure," Amos said. "Now, let's see how the next few weeks go. You've got to prove you can keep it up, you know."

Katie felt confident they could, especially since they had a common problem to overcome. They wondered if they should mention the mortgage situation to Amos but decided it would only complicate things. They were ready to give up some control to one another—but not to anyone else.

The next few days passed in a blur of activity. Katie crunched numbers, and Levi worked on ways to market the shop. Meanwhile, December swept into Bluebird Hills with a twinkling of *Englischer* lights and the sound of carols drifting from every shop on Main Street. Katie barely looked up from the confusing jumble of records Aunt Fannie had kept in the barn's tack room while Levi darted here and there, running errands and putting his plans into action. After a week, they came together to share their progress.

"Don't peek," Levi said. He led Katie by the elbow across the frozen earth and around the front of the shop. Simon skipped alongside them, darting ahead and doubling back impatiently. "I helped," Simon said. "I helped a lot."

Katie smiled and felt for her next step with the tip of her shoe. "I won't let you fall," Levi said. Katie felt his big, warm hands tighten around her arms, and she relaxed into them.

Katie heard the bark of a dog across the highway and the growl of a car engine whisking past. "Can I open my eyes yet?" she asked. The December air nipped at her cheeks.

"Okay," Simon shouted. "You can look!"

Katie opened her eyes to see a big sign in front of the shop, easily viewed from either direction of the highway. Actually, *big* wasn't the right word. It was huge.

"No one's going to miss that, ain't so?" Levi asked, hands on his hips as he gazed up at the bold lettering. Sadie stood beside the sign, looking at Katie expectantly.

Katie just stared. The sign read Aunt Fannie's Amish Gift Shop in giant red letters. Beneath the words were colorful images of assorted wares, from quilts and cookies to fresh vegetables and faceless Amish dolls.

"Sadie painted it," Simon said. "She did a really *gut* job, ain't so?"

Levi turned to Katie when she didn't respond. "Well, what do you think?"

"I…" Katie stumbled for the right words. She didn't want to hurt anybody's feelings, but it was so *bold*. Aunt Fannie never would have approved. She sensed a shift in the mood as everyone waited for her response. Sadie's hands tightened, and Levi's jaw twitched. "I think it's *wunderbaar*," Katie said quickly. "You're an incredible artist, Sadie."

Levi frowned, glanced at Sadie, then back at Katie. "You don't like it."

"I do," Katie said.

"It's okay," Sadie said. "We knew it was a risk. I know you're really traditional."

Katie flinched. "I'm Amish. Of course I'm traditional."

Sadie fiddled with one of the straight pins that fastened her dress. "What I meant was that you don't like change."

"Again, that goes with being Amish."

"Might be more than that with you, Katie," Levi said gently.

"Haven't you ever heard the expression *if it*

ain't broke, don't fix it?" Katie asked, her voice rising more than she meant it to.

Levi sighed and put a hand on Katie's shoulder. "But the situation *is* broken, Katie."

Katie paused. Everyone stared at her expectantly. "Okay," she muttered finally. "You're right. But…" Katie could not imagine looking at that enormous sign every day. There was nothing wrong with it—she didn't think it violated the *Ordnung*. But it just didn't feel right. It wasn't what she was used to. All those years she had waited to come back, dreaming that everything would be just as she had left it. She wanted to escape back into those happy childhood days and relive them.

But she wasn't a child anymore. And those days were gone.

"Sometimes new can be *gut*," Levi said quietly, his hand still firm and secure on her shoulder.

Katie shook her head. "Of course. I'm being silly. It's a *wunderbaar* sign. I just have to get used to the fact that Aunt Fannie's gift shop isn't really her gift shop anymore."

"Sure it is," Levi said. "It will always hold her memory and honor her." He gave her a meaningful look. "But only the past can stay in the past."

Katie giggled. "Whatever that means."

"I thought it sounded philosophical," Levi said with a grin.

A blue car on the highway slowed as the driver read the big sign. The blinker and the brake lights flicked on. Then the car made a sharp left turn into the driveway. Gravel crunched beneath the rubber tires.

"It's working!" Simon shouted. "They like the sign!"

Sadie glowed as an *Englisch* family poured out of the sedan. The father waved and asked if they were open.

"Ya," Katie said. "Come on in! We're so glad you stopped."

Levi nudged Katie in the ribs as she turned to follow the family inside. "Can't argue with results like that."

"Nee," she admitted. "Sure can't."

"Now just wait until you see what I do with the exterior."

Katie balked.

Levi raised his eyebrows and waited.

Katie groaned. "Okay. I trust you."

Levi winked. "You knew I was right all along."

"Don't push it," Katie said. She heard Levi chuckle as she walked away.

Katie and Sadie hunched over an assortment of paint samples while Eliza dusted a shelf of Christmas candles. "These shades of blue go well together," Sadie said as she tapped three different color strips.

"Those blues are very bright," Katie said.

"Ya," Sadie said. "That's kind of the point. We want people to notice the shop."

"I see you're keeping Katie on track," Levi's voice boomed from across the shop.

"Ach, Levi." Katie straightened up and stretched her back. "I didn't hear you come in."

"I've brought Gabriel to help set up a website."

Katie froze. "A website?"

"You heard me."

"Aenti Fannie never had a website."

"If I had a dollar for every time—"

"Okay, okay. I get it. But are you sure the bishop will be okay with it?"

"As long as it's for a business, our church district allows it," Levi said.

"So," Gabriel said as he stepped forward with a laptop tucked under his arm, "let's get started."

"You have a laptop?" Katie asked.

"Ya. Bought it when I started my *rumspringa."*

Eliza peered around the corner of a shelf with a curious expression on her face. "You actually know how to use that thing?"

"Sure. I sell my wood carvings online to make extra money. *Englischers* seem to like them."

Eliza did not go back to her work. Instead she stared at Gabriel and his high-tech contraption.

Gabriel sat on a stool and opened the laptop. A blue glow highlighted his features. "It's not that hard to create a website." He clicked the keyboard a few times, then turned the screen toward Katie. "See?"

"What's the point of having a website, anyway?"

Gabriel exhaled. "Sounds like we're going to have to start at the beginning."

"I'll brew some *kaffi*," Levi said. "We're both going to have a lot of questions."

Over the next few days, Levi was thrilled to see how quickly the run-down little shop transformed into a quaint tourist destination. They still had a long way to go before their profits would increase enough to make the back payments on the mortgage, but Levi felt sure they could get there. He and Gabriel spent hours repairing the woodwork and painting the exterior blue, white and pink, until the building looked like an oversize antique Victorian dollhouse. They trimmed the overgrown hedges lining the porch and strung greenery and simple white stars along the railing. Soon, the little building sparkled with holiday charm.

Levi leaned on his rake and nodded toward

the shop after the work was finally completed. "If that doesn't bring in customers, I don't know what will."

Katie stood with her hands on her hips, surveying the new look. She sighed.

"You hate it," Levi said as his stomach tightened.

"*Nee.* I love it."

"You're not acting like it."

"I guess I don't like being wrong."

"Ah. So you finally admit I was right about this makeover?"

"I wouldn't have let you do it if I didn't think it would attract customers."

"But it's more than that. You actually like it better than before."

Katie hesitated. "*Ya.* I admit, I like it better than before. You were right."

Levi pumped his fist in the air. "I knew it!"

"No, you didn't."

"Okay, you're right," Levi admitted. "I was terrified that you'd hate it."

"Terrified?" Katie asked in a teasing voice. "A big, strong man like you?"

"Hey, you can be pretty terrifying, even to a big, strong man like me."

Katie laughed and punched him playfully on the arm.

"Ouch," Levi said and rubbed his bicep.

"You deserve it. And anyway, if it really hurt, you wouldn't be grinning right now."

Levi chuckled. Before he realized what he was doing, he draped his arm around Katie's shoulder and pulled her closer. They stood side by side, looking at the shop and smiling. Levi's heart swelled as he stood with his arm around Katie, reveling in a sense of shared accomplishment. The moment felt so magical that he didn't want it to end. But as the rush of excitement faded, Levi began to feel awkward. He dropped his arm and stepped away from Katie. She straightened her apron and avoided his gaze. Her cheeks looked a shade redder than before.

"So," Levi said and kicked a pebble with the toe of his shoe. "What now?" He wondered if she was feeling what he was feeling. He wanted to share more moments like this with her. He wanted to feel her narrow shoulders beneath his arm again and see her smiling up at him. So what he really meant by *what now?* was *what happens with* us *now?* But he left the question open-ended to see how she would interpret it.

"Now I get to change the way you run the farm."

Levi's heart sank. Not because she wanted to change the farm. He didn't mind that too much now that he trusted her. His heart sank because she didn't respond by saying, *I'm ready to be more than friends.* But of course she didn't. That would be ridiculous and unprofessional. She would never suggest such a thing. Especially when they had more important matters to focus on.

Katie seemed surprised at how supportive Levi was about the changes she suggested. She had a lot of ideas on how to cut corners after crunching the numbers. Levi rubbed his chin between his thumb and forefinger as she went over each one, then nodded thoughtfully when she finished her list.

"*Gut,*" Levi said and nodded again. "Sounds *gut.*" He slapped his hand on the kitchen table and stood up. "I'll get started right away."

"Wait. That's it?"

Levi looked confused and sat back down. "Was there something else?"

"*Nee*... I just…" Katie shook her head and laughed. "Aren't you going to fight me on any of the suggestions I made?"

Levi raised his eyebrows. "Did you want me to?"

"*Nee.*" Katie laughed again. "Of course not."

Levi gave a sly smile. "You just can't handle that I'm better at teamwork than you are."

"Maybe I'm just shocked at what's come over you. Since when did you become so accommodating?"

"Since we became friends." Levi hesitated and shifted in his seat. "Since I realized how smart and capable you are."

Levi's eyes darted to the floor. He looked suddenly vulnerable in that moment, as if he was seeking her approval. Katie didn't know what to think. They had grown close over the last few weeks. She definitely thought of him as a friend. A good friend. And when he casually draped his arm around her or brushed his hand against hers, it always sent a jolt through her body that she couldn't explain. So she felt flustered by his unexpected compliment—and by the sheepish way he acted afterward. Was he hinting that he admired her as more than a friend?

Nee. That didn't make sense. Levi was nothing like her. Their personalities went together about as well as oil and water. They were finally getting along as business partners, but that didn't mean he felt anything for her beyond that. Levi was probably just relieved that she had stopped giving him a hard time. *Being friends with Levi is gut,* Katie told herself. *But anything more than that would be asking for trouble.*

If only the strange, unexpected longing in her chest would agree with her logic.

Katie focused her attention on the paper in her hand and tried to shake thoughts of Levi out of her mind. "I also wanted to talk to you about organic farming."

"Okay." Levi leaned back in the kitchen chair. "I'm listening."

"It's more expensive and labor-intensive to farm that way, but I ran the numbers and I think that we will earn more in the long run."

She turned the paper around and slid it across the table. Levi studied the lines of numbers and nodded. "I don't need to see the figures," Levi said after a moment. "I trust you."

Katie's eyes jerked to his. "You do?"

His warm brown gaze melted into her. "*Ya.* Of course."

Katie swallowed hard. Knowing that he trusted her made her feel a rush of excitement. And the way he stared into her eyes felt deeper than just friendship...

Levi broke eye contact and grinned that impish smile of his. "Plus, I hate math. So I'll leave all that to you."

Katie frowned and looked back at the paper. Levi always turned a serious moment into a joke. Maybe it had never been serious for him in the first place. Maybe she was just imagining things because she was falling for him.

Falling for him! Had that thought really just formed inside her mind? She shifted in her seat and deepened her frown. She had to get control of her thoughts and emotions. Katie glanced up, saw Levi watching her and felt herself blush. She dropped her eyes back to the paper and cleared her throat. "So," she said in a shaky voice. "*Englischers* love organic produce. They pay top prices for it."

"Okay. It'll take some time to make the changes. We'll do the research and aim to get started next season with some of the produce."

Katie nodded. "Sounds reasonable. I just wish we could make changes faster than that. I worry it might be too late by then."

Levi rubbed his beard thoughtfully. "Farming is a slow business. Can't control that."

"Feels like we can't control much," Katie said.

Levi studied her expression for a moment. "And you like to be in control, ain't so?"

"Doesn't everyone?"

"Sure," Levi said. "But some more than others."

Katie laughed awkwardly. "And I guess I fall into the 'some' category."

"Reckon so. I figure you didn't have much control over how your life played out until now. Sounds like you were pretty much stuck in a situation without a way to fix it."

"I wasn't unhappy. I mean, I was glad to be able to help my family."

"I know." Levi paused and studied Katie's

expression. "But you didn't really feel like you had a choice, did you?"

Katie considered that for a moment. *"Nee."*

"So even though you were glad to help, you didn't actually choose that path for your life. And you couldn't control your mother's illness. It's hard to watch someone you love suffer and not be able to fix it."

Katie was surprised how well Levi understood her. She felt like he was reading her from the inside, like a book that no one else had bothered to open. *"Ya."* She picked at the hem of her apron. "You're right. It's very hard."

"Now you want to control whatever you can," Levi said. "It's understandable."

"Understandable, but not helpful," Katie replied.

"Don't be too hard on yourself. I've had to get over that need for control, too, you know."

"You mean when your wife—" Katie shook her head. "Sorry. I didn't mean to overstep."

Levi exhaled. "No. It's *oll recht.* You're right. After Rachel died, I wanted everything to be perfect for Simon. I wanted to control our lives, make a perfect sanctuary for us where nothing bad could ever happen again."

Katie instinctively reached out and put her hand over Levi's. "I think you still feel driven to do that." His hand felt warm and callused beneath hers. She wanted to reassure him that everything would be okay, but she was surprised by how much the touch of his hand reassured *her* instead. She felt stronger inside knowing they were in this together.

Levi gave a dry chuckle and looked into her eyes. "I guess we're not so different after all, for all our bickering."

"We haven't bickered in a long time," Katie said quietly, still looking into his eyes.

Levi's face dropped back into a serious expression as they gazed at one another. "No," he said. "We haven't."

Katie wondered if he felt as connected to her as she did to him at that moment. Then his fingers tightened around her hand and she knew the answer.

"Hey, *Daed*!" Simon shot into the kitchen carrying a mason jar in his hand.

Katie and Levi jerked their hands apart, the moment fracturing at the intrusion. Levi's expression quickly shifted to a big grin for his son. "What do you have there?"

"One of my caterpillars is coming out of his cocoon!"

"That's great," Levi said. "Come sit and we can all watch together."

Simon skipped to the table with a delighted

look on his face. "Just wait till you see him, *Daed*. He's going to be beautiful, ain't so?"

"I'm sure he is."

"But don't you have to go work?" Simon asked as he slid into a chair and set the glass jar onto the table with a thump. "It's not supper time yet."

Katie answered before Levi could. "Sometimes we need to take time to do more important things," she said.

Levi's eyes met hers, and he gave a warm smile. "You don't think we need to get started on this list right away?"

"I think we need to get started on it soon, but this is more important for right now."

"Why, Katie Schwartz, if I didn't know any better, I'd think you were letting yourself give up a little bit of control and relax."

"I'm full of surprises, Levi Miller."

Levi's smile faded into a thoughtful expression as his deep brown eyes stayed on hers. "You certainly are," he said softly.

And Katie realized there was no place she would rather be than right there, in the old, weathered kitchen with Levi and Simon, spending a spontaneous moment together…like a family.

Chapter Ten

Levi whistled as he worked. Everything was going according to plan. Katie's ideas were great, and he knew they could make a real difference. He had already managed to implement quite a few of her suggestions. Now he was tackling the big white barn. Katie had not mentioned it, but it was obviously in need of a fresh coat of paint. The weathered clapboards were peeling and created a shoddy view from the gift shop's parking lot. A fresh coat of paint would do loads of good—especially since he had chosen a bright red. Simon had gone to the paint store with him and helped him pick out the perfect color. Now, when tourists pulled into the property, they would see an idyllic red barn that looked like something straight out of the pages of a children's book.

"This is going to take ages, you know," Gabriel grumbled from the ladder beside Levi.

"Days," Levi corrected. "Not ages."

"It will feel like ages," Gabriel said.

"It will be worth it," Levi said as he strained to reach a spot he had missed. He wasn't daunted by the task ahead. Amish were expected to work hard—it was a way of life for him.

"Ya," Gabriel said. "It'll look *gut*. The tourists will take lots of selfies in front of it and post them to social media, which will be like free advertising."

"Is that right?" Levi asked as he dipped his brush in the bucket of red paint hanging from the ladder. "Can't understand why anyone would want to take a photo of themselves. Kind of blocks the view, ain't so?"

Gabriel laughed. "Not everything the *Englisch* do makes sense. I thought it was a little weird, too, when I first got a smartphone. But then I got used to it, and it seems normal now. That's the way these things work, *ya*? You see enough of something and eventually it isn't weird anymore."

Levi furrowed his brows. "Some things shouldn't seem normal. Putting so much attention on oneself isn't *gut*."

Gabriel shrugged. "Maybe not. But it's what people do." He took a moment to swipe his brush across a long section of clapboard. "Has business picked up since you've made all the improvements around here?"

"Ya," Levi said. "We're getting a lot more people into the shop than we used to. There're not all buying, but at least they're coming in. Hopefully—"

"What are you doing!" Katie shrieked from across the farmyard. Levi cringed. What had he done this time?

Slowly putting down the paintbrush, he craned his neck to look down at the ground behind him. Katie stood with her hands on her hips, face red, her mouth puckered into a tight line. "Something wrong?" Levi asked as calmly as he could.

"You're painting the barn red!"

"Ya. Looks nice, ain't so? Just like a postcard."

"But it's red!"

Levi sighed again. "All right. I'm coming down." He slid his hands along the cool metal sides of the ladder as he carefully picked his way down the rungs. He jumped the last two and landed on the ground. "What's so bad about red?"

"The fact that it's not white!"

Levi took off his hat and scratched his head. "No, it's definitely not white."

"Don't patronize me, Levi Miller." Katie's

face turned a brighter shade of scarlet. She looked about to spit fire.

Levi held up his hands, palms outward. "Just stating the facts."

"The *facts* are that you're ruining the barn. You had no right! You didn't ask me. You didn't even mention it!"

Levi wanted to be patient and talk through whatever Katie's problem was, but her attitude cut to the quick. "Now, just a minute," he said, his voice rising to a low growl. "I've put a lot of time and effort into this. And it looks *gut*. The tourists will love it. You should be thanking me."

"Thanking you?" Katie's eyes narrowed as her voice tightened. "*Thanking* you? Ha! For what? Taking a perfectly *gut* barn and making it look like...like...*that*!" She pointed an accusatory finger at the section of barn painted bright, bold red.

"So does this mean we get to stop?" Gabriel asked from the top of his ladder.

Levi and Katie both swiveled their faces to him. "No!" Levi shouted at the same time that Katie yelled, "Yes!"

Gabriel chuckled, set down his brush and scampered down the ladder. "*Gut* time for a snack break, ain't so?" he said to himself and headed for the farmhouse kitchen.

Katie turned back to Levi. "Fix this," she demanded.

"Not on your life," Levi said. "It looks *gut* and I'm going to finish it. No matter how ungrateful you are about it."

"Ungrateful?" Katie snorted. "Ungrateful!"

"*Ya.* That's the word for it."

"How dare you?"

"How dare I fix up this old run-down place so we can turn a profit and keep it? *Ya*, I'm a real monster, all right."

Katie narrowed her eyes, then spun around on her heel and stomped away.

Levi watched her go, pulse pounding against his temples. How could she come after him like that? Didn't she see how hard he was working to keep the farm and make her happy?

Levi flinched.

Was that why he felt so angry? Because he was trying to make her happy? Deep down, beneath that anger, was he actually feeling rejected? This was supposed to be about improving the business, not impressing some woman as if they were courting. Right?

Levi watched Katie stalk across the farmyard. A speckled hen squawked and flapped its wings as she hurried past, then attacked her black leather shoe. Katie stumbled, then straightened up, obviously trying to look dignified. She glanced over her shoulder to see if Levi had seen, then scowled and whipped her head back around.

Levi felt the anger melt away in that moment. Katie looked so vulnerable as she struggled to regain her dignity. Her actions toward him had been uncalled-for—*very* uncalled-for—but she was clearly hurting inside, and Levi couldn't allow that. Even if she *had* blamed him unjustly. "Katie, wait!" he called after her.

Katie kept walking.

"Katie!" Levi repeated as he took off after her.

She stopped but didn't turn around as he jogged to reach her. Her shoulders rose and fell as she took a deep breath and released it. Levi circled around to face her and was shocked to see tears glittering in her eyes. She quickly wiped them away in an angry gesture.

"I'm sorry." Levi put a hand on each of her upper arms and looked her in the eyes. "I don't know what I did that hurt you so much, but whatever it was, I'm sorry."

"Nee." Katie shook her head. "You didn't do anything. It's me, not you."

Levi was tempted to make a playful wise-crack at that comment, but he didn't. He didn't want to put up any barriers between them by downplaying the moment. He wanted to tear all the barriers down.

"I'm the one who should be sorry." Katie wiped her eyes with the back of her brown woolen mitten. "You didn't do anything wrong."

Levi kept his gaze steady and firm as he looked into her hazel eyes. "Tell me what you're feeling. Why are you so upset?"

"I don't know. Something just came over me. So much has changed around here over the last few weeks, and when I saw the barn was changing, too, it felt like my last memories of *Aenti* Fannie and my childhood were disappearing. It just felt like too much all the sudden."

Levi nodded. "I understand."

"Even so, I shouldn't have yelled at you like that. Especially when you were trying to do the right thing." She squeezed her eyes shut and shook her head. "Not just trying—*doing* the right thing." Katie reopened her eyes. "It's really hard to admit, but the barn does look a lot better. It needed a fresh coat of paint. And as much as I want it to stay the same color it has always been, the tourists would rather see a red barn."

"Thanks for saying so. Apology accepted. I'm sorry I yelled back. And I'm sorry I didn't consult you first. I guess I just got used to you going along with all the changes and took it for granted that you'd be okay with it, especially since it's part of the farm and not the shop." Levi looked down and scuffed the dirt with the toe of his work boot. "I guess I was excited to see your reaction. I wanted to surprise you."

"It's a huge barn. You couldn't keep it a secret while you paint it."

Levi felt sheepish. "*Nee*, but I thought it would make you happy to walk outside and see a portion of it painted red, even though it wouldn't be finished yet. I thought you'd like it."

Katie froze. "You...wanted to make me happy?"

Levi kept his eyes on the ground. "*Ya*. I did."

She hesitated, then asked in a small voice, "Why?"

Levi tugged at the collar of his shirt. He felt hot and stuffy all the sudden. "Because, uh, I guess, well, I like the way your face lights up when you smile. You have the most *wunderbaar* smile. Your face shines like a little girl on Christmas morning, despite how serious and businesslike you always act."

"You wanted to see me smile?" A little crease formed between Katie's eyebrows, as though she was trying to process what he was telling her.

Levi swallowed hard. He was sure he had said the wrong thing. *"Ya."* He hesitated, then added, "I guess that's pretty *narrisch*."

Fresh tears sparkled in Katie's eyes. "That isn't *narrisch*, Levi. It's the sweetest thing anyone's ever said to me. And I'm so glad you said it."

Levi's head shot up. "You are?"

"*Ya*. I am."

"But we're, um, business partners," Levi said.

"*Ya*. We are."

Their words hung in the frosty air as they stared into one another's eyes. Levi could her his heartbeat in the silence.

"So what happens now?" Katie finally asked, her lips trembling slightly. Levi didn't know if it was from cold or emotion. He hoped it was from emotion. Either way, he had to take a risk and release what was burning within him.

"We become more than business partners," Levi answered quietly.

Katie sucked in a breath. Seconds ticked by. Levi's pulse pounded in his throat as he waited for her response.

She nodded slowly, seemingly unable to verbalize her thoughts.

Levi felt a rush of joy that shot all the way down to his toes. He grabbed her hand, lifted it to his lips and kissed her fingers through the mittens, then squeezed her hand. "This means more change, you know," he said as he kept his gaze firmly on hers.

Katie swallowed hard and nodded again. "I know," she said. "But sometimes change is *gut*. Isn't that what you've taught me?"

Levi felt his heart swell with emotion for the woman standing in front of him. "*Ya*. This change will definitely be *gut*. I promise you that."

Katie couldn't believe what was happening. Aunt Fannie must have planned this all along. Amos and Edna might have been in on it, too— or had suspected, at least. No wonder Amos had made that cryptic comment that she might be surprised how things turned out. Katie should have guessed her wily old aunt would hatch a secret matchmaking plan as a final gift.

Even wilder was that it had actually worked.

The next week passed in a blur of excitement. Simon seemed to sense the new, positive energy between Katie and Levi. The little boy laughed more and spent more time with the two of them. He loved to plop down on the sofa with a book in hand, wiggle his way between them and insist they all look at the photos of animals together.

Katie had never been happier than in those moments. That surprised her, because hard work and the sense of accomplishment that came with it had always been what fulfilled her. Suddenly, to her amazement, the shop was no longer the most important thing in her life.

The change was obvious enough that Eliza noticed, even though Katie said nothing about her and Levi's fledgling relationship.

"You haven't stopped grinning all week," Eliza said as she dusted a shelf of homemade canned goods on Friday afternoon.

Katie's eyes jerked up from the ledger where she had been studying the shop's overhead for the last month. "Oh? I hadn't noticed."

Eliza gave a little harrumph as she moved the feather duster over a mason jar labeled Apple Butter. "Hard not to." A knowing smile curled the corner of her lips. "You're not the only one who can't stop grinning, you know."

Katie shifted in her seat. "*Ach*, I'm sure I don't know who you're talking about."

Eliza stopped dusting, put her hands on her hips and raised an eyebrow. "I'm sure you do."

Katie swallowed hard. Eliza was younger than her, but Eliza's rigid demeanor always made Katie feel like she was under the scrutiny of a church elder.

When Katie didn't respond, Eliza continued by adding, "It's *gut* to see Levi happy again."

"*Ach*, well…" Eliza had become a friend and not just an employee, but Katie wasn't good at sharing her feelings. Besides, Amish courtships were typically carried out privately. It wasn't uncommon for the church district to be surprised when courting couples announced an engagement. So, instead of responding, Katie just stared at Eliza awkwardly.

Eliza seemed flustered by Katie's silence. She cleared her throat, pushed her glasses up the bridge of her nose and resumed dusting. "I didn't mean to pry. But it's obvious, ain't so? And you two seem right for each other. It's a *gut* match. Levi has always seemed set on remaining a widower, but *Gott* has plans we can't see, *ya*?"

"Except for Fannie," Katie said. "She was in on it, for certain sure."

They both laughed. Then Eliza's expression softened into a wistful smile. "I don't like to admit it, but I'm a romantic at heart. There's nothing like a happy ending."

Katie studied the faraway gleam in Eliza's eyes. "I never would have guessed."

"Well, we all have our secrets, don't we? You and Levi certainly did. Falling for each other, right under our noses, all the while acting as though you weren't the least bit interested in one another."

"*Ach*, I wasn't pretending. I don't think he was, either."

"Mmm." Eliza seemed lost in thought for a moment as she ran the feather duster along a jar of peach jelly. Then her face shifted back to its usual no-nonsense expression and the dreamy look in her eyes faded. "So what happens now that you're walking out together? Have you made plans for the future?" Eliza lifted the mason jar and dusted around it. "You already share the property. Seems like everything's all set to wrap up pretty nicely, ain't so?"

Katie's stomach tightened. She wondered if she was doing the right thing to keep the truth about the possible foreclosure from everyone. But it was Katie's and Levi's responsibility to fix the problem. Telling Eliza so close to Christmas would only cause needless worry. "I, uh, well, we haven't really made any plans," Katie mumbled. That was true. The realization pulled her out of the clouds and back to reality.

What did Levi envision for them? He certainly had not proposed or even mentioned marriage yet. How could he when they might lose their home and livelihood in just a few weeks?

"I expect you'll get a proposal any day now," Eliza said as she moved from the canned goods to a stack of Sadie's off-white scarves. Eliza paused to refold one of the scarves. "No reason for Levi to wait."

"Ya." Katie turned away so Eliza couldn't see the concern on her face. Her fingers fumbled over the ledger as she tried to find her place.

The bell rang as the shop door swung open and Levi swept inside with a blast of cold air and three mugs of hot chocolate.

Eliza looked at Katie and raised her eyebrows in a *look who's here* expression. "Can't stay away," she whispered.

Levi managed to grip the handles of two mugs at once in his left hand, and he held another in his right, barely managing to keep the liquid from sloshing over the top as he walked to the counter. "Thought you could use a little pick-me-up," he said with a friendly wink and set one of the mugs in front of Katie.

"You look like you could use one yourself," Katie replied. His nose was red, his fingers raw.

Levi gave a crooked smile and leaned a hip against the counter. "It's mighty cold out there. Had to spend the morning in the bottom field, where the wind rips right through you."

Eliza looked expectantly at Levi. "Is that one for me?"

"Sure is," Levi said. "Come get it while it's hot."

Eliza dropped the feather duster and hurried over. *"Danki."*

Levi nodded and blew across the top of his mug. "Looks *gut* in here," he said. Katie had just arranged fresh evergreen boughs, holly branches and red candles in the windows and along the display tables. Levi breathed in deeply through his nose. "Smells like a pine forest."

"You don't think it's too much, do you?" Eliza asked with a little frown as she gripped her mug in both hands.

"Too much?" Levi shook his head and chuckled. "Not at all. It's not like you have a Christmas tree in here or anything like that."

"*Nee*, of course not." Eliza looked scandalized.

"It would probably be allowed," Levi said. "For business. To display the ornaments."

"Better not to push it," she said with a sniff.

Levi nodded. "You don't need to, anyway. It looks perfect in here." His eyes roamed the shelves for a moment, and Katie sensed that he was thinking about more than he was saying.

"What is it?" she asked as she took a small sip of the piping-hot chocolate.

Levi puffed up his cheeks and exhaled. "Uh, I was just thinking…" He frowned, glanced at Eliza, then moved his attention to Katie. "Just wondering…"

Levi seemed nervous. Did he want to talk about their relationship? Clearly, he wanted to speak in private. The thought made her stomach jump.

"I was just wondering if you wanted to ride to town with me. I've got to run some errands.

Maybe you have some shopping of your own to do?"

Katie leaped up. "*Ya*. I do. This is *gut* timing." She felt flustered and excited to spend some time alone with just Levi, no distractions. They rarely had that opportunity. It wouldn't be appropriate for them to be alone in the house together, of course, but going out in a buggy unchaperoned was acceptable. Katie turned to Eliza. "If you can manage, that is?"

"Of course. And there's a list of items we need for the shop." Eliza nodded toward a yellow notepad on the counter.

Katie tore the top sheet from the notepad and stuffed the paper in her pocket. "*Danki*. Be back soon."

"No need to hurry," Eliza said. Katie was sure the woman had an impish twinkle in her eye, even though it was completely out of character. If felt good to know that someone was rooting for her and Levi, even if Katie did feel awkward and uncomfortable sharing her complicated personal life.

"Better bundle up," Levi said as he grabbed Katie's black winter coat from the rack. "It's cold out there." She shivered at his warm, gentle touch as he helped her into the coat, then glanced up at his eyes. This was going to be a *wunderbaar* afternoon.

* * *

A soft, white snow began to fall as the buggy wheels crunched over gravel, then rolled onto the main road to whine against the pavement. Biscuit's breath puffed upward in little white clouds as they plodded past rolling brown fields and bales of hay. Katie rubbed her hands together to warm them against the biting cold. Levi glanced over at her. "Forgot your mittens?"

"Ya."

"Here," he said. He kept one hand on the reins, lifted the other hand to his mouth and tugged a glove off with his teeth. "Put this on."

"But you'll freeze."

Levi shrugged. "I'll be all right." He removed the other glove and tossed it in her lap.

Katie slid her hands into the heavy black gloves, still warm from his body heat. They looked comically large on her hands. Levi glanced at them and chuckled. "Cute," he murmured.

"Levi?" Katie asked, then bit her lip.

"Ya?"

"I thought you might have something to ask me."

Levi exhaled. "Right."

Katie waited, heart hammering with expectation. Biscuit's hooves clattered against the asphalt as snowflakes pirouetted from the sky to land on Katie's face. They stuck to her eyelashes, and she blinked, then shivered. Levi leaned over and tucked the lap blanket more tightly around her. Katie watched him expectantly. Would he ask her to marry him? He seemed nervous enough. No, there were too many complications for that right now…and yet… An eager smile curled the corners of her lips.

"I've been wanting to ask about the sales so far this month," Levi said.

Katie felt herself deflate like a balloon. "Of course." This wasn't a romantic buggy ride in the snow. It was a business meeting.

Which was fine. They needed to discuss the business. She had just hoped…

"You *oll recht*?" Levi asked.

"*Ya*. I'm fine." She hoped the disappointment didn't show on her face. "Just thinking about the question."

"Is it that bad?"

"Um…" Katie straightened in her seat and furrowed her brow. She had to switch gears and start thinking business. "Well, it's not *gut*."

"Exactly how not *gut*?"

"We've got more people coming in—the tourists seem to love the shop's new look, and the marketing is definitely helping—but they're not buying enough. At this rate we're not going to be able to stop the foreclosure."

"How short are we?"

Levi responded with a low whistle when Katie told him the dollar amount.

They rode in silence for a moment, watching a blanket of white slowly descend over Bluebird Hills. The light layer of snow dusted split-rail fences, fields of winter wheat and weathered barns. Biscuit's bay coat was damp from snowflakes melted by her body heat. In the distance, children dragged a sled up a hill and shouted to one another, their eager, high-pitched voices carrying through the brisk winter air.

"Any thoughts on why they're not buying the wares?" Levi asked finally.

Katie frowned. "No."

Levi studied her face for a moment before turning his attention back to the road. "You sure about that?"

Katie's frowned deepened. "Why would you ask me that?"

"The look on your face."

Katie grunted. A snowflake landed on her cheek, and she brushed it away. They passed an *Englischer* house decorated with Christmas lights that glowed green against the gray sky. "I don't know. Maybe."

"I think you know what needs to be done."

Katie whipped her head toward Levi. "What do you mean by that?"

Levi kept his eyes straight ahead. "I bet there's something new you need to try, but you don't want to do it."

Katie's eyes narrowed. "Why would you think that?"

"Because I know you. You don't like change. And you're too savvy not to have some idea of what needs to be changed. That means you probably know what to do, you just don't want to face it."

Katie exhaled between her teeth. "Humph."

Levi chuckled. "That's all you've got to say?"

"Ya."

"Sounds like I'm right."

"Don't push it, Levi Miller."

Levi chuckled again. "Okay, okay." A few beats passed, punctuated by the clatter of horse hooves on pavement. Levi's expression softened. "Want to share?" he asked gently. "I'd like to help."

"No. But we're in this together, so I guess I should."

"I'm sure it's not as bad as redoing the shop's exterior or painting the barn red."

Katie sighed. *"Aenti* Fannie would have a fit."

"Maybe not," Levi said. "Maybe she would want you to make the shop your own. Put your own mark on it, make it successful again."

Katie pondered that for a moment.

"So, what is it that you need to do?"

"I think I need to sell something different. Something that will make us stand out from the all the other Amish gift shops in Lancaster County. We need to offer stuff that tempts the tourists to make impulse buys."

"Cream-colored scarves not tempting enough?" Levi glanced over at her with a crooked little grin.

Katie laughed. "Off-white. But *ya*, you're right. Not enough customers want them."

"What about the candles? They smell mighty *gut*."

Katie shrugged. "They're nice, but you can get scented Christmas candles anywhere."

Levi nodded. "So what's your solution?"

"I don't know, exactly. But I think the best place to start is to see what Sadie's offering to sell. I know she's a *gut* artist after seeing the sign she painted."

"I thought we already sold her stuff."

"We do. But she mentioned that she has some artwork to offer. Eliza's against it, so I dismissed the idea. I was afraid of putting anything in the shop that was…"

"Too bold? Too different?"

"Exactly."

Levi shot her a look. "You know that's exactly what you need in order to get impulse buys."

Katie considered that for a moment. "*Ya*.

You're probably right. It's risky, but I think I better see what she has to offer, at least." She glanced at Levi with a concerned look. "But I'm afraid the church district might be against it. They already think I'm the villain who's after your land."

Levi laughed. "Don't mind Viola. She means well. No one thinks you're a villain."

Katie raised an eyebrow.

"Okay, okay, maybe some people were concerned at first. But you've more than proven yourself since then."

"Glad to hear you admit that, Levi Miller."

"Any time, Katie Schwartz."

Katie giggled. "You know, I thought *you* were the villain."

"Oh, believe me, I know," Levi said, and they both laughed.

They passed a herd of cows huddled beneath a bare oak tree in a white-coated field. Wind whipped through the branches and scattered a handful of dry, brown leaves. Katie's pensive mood returned as she studied the bleak landscape.

"What is it?" Levi asked. "Where did that frown come from all the sudden?"

"I was just thinking about the gift shop and all the changes we're having to make. Don't you ever want to go back and keep everything the way it used to be?"

Levi paused. Biscuit's hooves clattered against the pavement in a steady rhythm. "I did," Levi said, all laughter gone from his voice. "I spent years wishing that. But if that happened, I wouldn't be here with you." His Adam's apple bobbed as he swallowed. "I don't pretend to understand *Gott*'s plans. But I'm beginning to realize He has *gut* things in store for us—if we hold on long enough."

Katie was filled with warmth despite the frigid air. She felt a sense of rightness settle deep within her. "You're talking about more than the shop," she whispered.

"*Ya.* I am."

Katie looked at Levi's hands as they gripped the reins. His bare fingers were red and stiff from the cold because he had sacrificed his gloves to keep her hands warm. "It's been hard to let go," Katie said. "I always had an idea of what it would be like to come back here. I dreamed about it for years. It was all planned out in my head."

"But reality isn't something you can plan."

"No." Katie put a hand on Levi's sleeve. She could feel the solid muscles of his forearm through his heavy winter coat. "I couldn't have planned this." Her gesture conveyed a deeper meaning to her words. "So I'm not sorry that everything is different than I dreamed it would be. Not anymore."

Levi's eyes softened. Then he said, "Except for the fact that the business is about to go under."

Katie chuckled at his bluntness. "*Ya*, that I could do without. I don't know if it will make a difference, but I'll talk to Sadie first thing tomorrow.

Levi nodded. "And, if you don't mind, I could speak to Gabriel. He says his wood carvings do pretty well online. Might do well in the shop, too."

"*Oll recht.* Why not?" Katie shook her head. "I can only imagine what change will come next."

"That's okay, because *Gott* already knows."

The buggy clattered onto Bluebird Hill's Main Street, where red and green Christmas lights glimmered through the heavy white snowfall. The row of quaint shops lined the way, windows glowing yellow in the dim, cloud-covered afternoon. A majestic pine tree strung with lights and silver balls towered over a corner bakery and bookshop. The green branches shimmered with white snowflakes.

Katie stared at the wintry scene in wonder. "It looks like a different world with the fresh-fallen snow," she murmured.

Levi tugged the reins, and the buggy shuddered to a stop beneath the giant Christmas tree. He flashed Katie an encouraging grin. "Everything looks different when you have a fresh perspective."

Chapter Eleven

Katie paid Sadie a visit the next morning while
Eliza watched the shop. She heard the shouts of
children and the rumble of adult voices through
the walls of the Lapps' yellow farmhouse as she
stood on the front porch. A small, pale face appeared at a window as soon as she knocked. Katie
waved at the little girl, who quickly ducked out
of sight. The door swung open, and Ada stood
in the threshold, wiping her hands on her apron.
"What a pleasant surprise, Katie. *Kumme* in."
She stepped back and motioned Katie inside. "I
was just pouring the *kaffi* while some of the *kinner* finished breakfast. Please join us."

Katie stomped her snowy boots on the door-
mat, then stepped into a warm entry hall lined
with nine pairs of shoes and nine coats in assorted sizes. The smell of bacon and strong,
dark-roast *kaffi* met her.

"*Danki*, but I can only stay a few minutes. I have to get back to the shop. Is Sadie here? I was hoping to speak with her."

"*Ya*. She's been helping the *kinner* get ready for school. Sadie?" Ada hollered up the staircase at the end of the entry hall. "You've got company."

A moment later, footsteps pounded down the steps and Sadie bounded into the room. "Hi!" She looked surprised but pleased to see Katie.

"I've got to keep the *kinner* moving so they're not late for school," Ada said as she headed for the kitchen. "*Kumme*, get *kaffi* before you go," she added before disappearing through the threshold.

"I know you're busy, so I'll make this quick," Katie said.

"It's all right." Sadie laughed. "It's always busy around here."

Katie smiled. "I bet so. I had my hands full with my younger sisters when I was your age, too."

Sadie's eyes brightened. "You did?"

"*Ya*. They're old enough to look after themselves now. But I remember the chaos of school mornings."

"*Daed* likes to keep things quiet, orderly and predictable, so I try…" Sadie shook her head and laughed again. "But it's just not possible with six *kinner* in the *haus*."

As if on cue, something crashed in the kitchen, and a child howled.

"I'll be there in a minute!" Sadie said loudly enough to be heard in the next room.

"I've been thinking about the artwork that you wanted to sell at my shop," Katie said. "I'd like to see it."

Sadie gasped. "You mean…"

Katie nodded. "Bring your work over today, if you can. All of it. I can't pay you up front, though. If I like it, would you mind selling on consignment?"

"Ya!" She rocked up onto the toes of her shoes and down again. "I mean, *nee*, I don't mind! Thank you, Katie!" She hesitated, then added, "I didn't think you were interested. What made you change your mind?"

Katie wondered what to say and decided there was nothing wrong with being straightforward. "We need to increase sales. And, after seeing what you did with the sign and with the color scheme for the exterior of the shop, I think you might be the way to do that."

"Wow." Sadie looked stunned. She put a hand on the banister to steady herself. "That's a *wunderbaar* thing to hear. I just hope I can live up to your expectations."

"I'm sure you will," Katie said with an encouraging grin.

"You do understand that my art is...creative? It doesn't violate the *Ordnung*, but it's not always what people expect from an Amish woman."

"I gathered that from what Eliza has said."

Sadie let out a deep breath. "Okay, I'll gather everything I've made and *kumme* over to the shop as soon as I can get away.

"Can't wait to see it all," Katie said. "Oh, and tell your *mamm* I'm sorry I can't stay for *kaffi*. I need to get back to the shop."

Sadie pressed her hands together. "I'm so excited I can hardly wait. See you soon!"

"See you," Katie said as she headed back outside. The frosty morning air stung her bare cheeks and made her eyes water. Pulling her coat tighter around her, she cut across the field that separated her property from the Lapps'. Fresh snow crunched beneath her boots. Rays of sun sparkled against the stark white landscape as she trudged through the drifts, a fresh surge of hope pushing her onward. If Sadie's artwork sold well, then maybe, just maybe... Katie broke into a smile, then took a deep, cleansing breath of the refreshing winter air. Now that she had a plan, everything felt better—more in control. A vague thought tickled the back of her brain— something about giving up control—but she pushed it away. It felt so good to see a way out of her and Levi's dilemma. Everything would be okay now.

It had to be.

Eliza was not so positive. "You did what?" she asked with her arms crossed as Katie dismantled a display of Christmas candles at the front of the store.

"I told Sadie we would sell the rest of her stuff."

Eliza's lips tightened into a line, and she shook her head.

Katie didn't respond as she rearranged the candles on a nearby shelf, intertwining the glass jars with sprigs of holly and ivy.

"She makes things that aren't Plain," Eliza said after a long, tense moment of silence. "Besides, I thought you were against changing the way Fannie did things."

"I am." Katie shook her head. "I mean, I was." She frowned as she smoothed a wrinkle from the white runner beneath the candles and greenery. "But we're not selling much."

"We're getting by. We always do."

Christmas was almost here. The last thing Katie wanted was to ruin Eliza's holiday by telling her the bad news. That could wait until the new year.

And, even though Katie didn't want to admit

it, she didn't like the idea of sharing her problems. She would rather keep it between her and Levi. Katie was used to being independent. She had always relied on herself when *Mamm* was sick and she had to raise her younger sisters.

Katie kept her thoughts to herself and switched the subject back to Sadie. "What Sadie makes might not be Plain, but she's not going to display it in her own home. Some Amish men do fancy woodworking for *Englisch* houses, but they would never install decorative molding in their own living rooms. I figure it's the same thing, really."

Eliza paused a moment. "Well, I suppose that makes sense. Kind of. But I still don't like it. I don't want to encourage Sadie to be too creative. She comes close enough to breaking the *Ordnung* without our help."

"It took me a long time to warm up to the idea, you know." Katie threw up her hands. "But what else can we do?"

Eliza looked at Katie strangely. Her eyes narrowed behind her big, round glasses. Katie realized she had said too much.

"What do you mean—"

The front door blew open, and Sadie bustled into the shop with a giant smile and a large wooden crate in her arms. Her cheeks were flushed from cold and excitement. "I've brought everything I have. I hope you like it." Her eyes glanced up at Katie nervously.

"Let's take a look," Katie said, ignoring the way Eliza raised her eyebrows. She lifted from the crate a framed mosaic that depicted the star of Bethlehem shining over the peaceful village. Bright, brilliant shards of colored glass were skillfully interwoven into complex patterns to create a symphony of colors and textures. Katie lifted the mosaic up to the sunlight shining through the shop windows, making the colors glow softly in her hands. She took in every detail, every clever use of pattern and design.

"You don't like them," Sadie murmured.

"*Nee.* I do." She shook her head. "I just don't know what to say. It's so creative."

"Perhaps a little too creative," Eliza muttered. Sadie flinched.

"There's nothing wrong with these," Katie said quickly. "I mean, I don't think it breaks any of our rules for you to make these to sell to tourists." She turned one of the mosaics slowly in her hands. The glass glimmered as she studied the intricate, geometric design. "How did you…?" Katie ran her finger over the smooth surface. "You taught yourself, didn't you?"

"*Ya.*"

Katie set down the mosaic, pulled a canvas from the crate and sucked in her breath. "This will sell for sure and certain!" The oil painting depicted rolling farmland in the wintertime, but instead of the expected colors, Sadie had used only shades of blue. It made Katie feel thoughtful and sad and nostalgic all at the same time. "This is…" She sighed and studied the brushstrokes. "…amazing."

Eliza peered at the painting over the top of her glasses. "I don't know why everything is blue."

"Because it makes you feel…" Katie hesitated. "I don't know how to explain it. It makes me feel sad, but in a *gut* way that feels peaceful and sweet."

Sadie bit her lip and looked down.

"Did I say the wrong thing?" Katie asked.

"Nee." Sadie raised her eyes, and Katie saw that they were shining. "No one's ever said that about my paintings before. No one understands them."

"Because they're blue," Eliza said matter-of-factly.

"Eliza," Katie said firmly.

Eliza sniffed. "I'm just pointing out the obvious."

"Art isn't about the obvious," Sadie said softly.

"Nee," Katie agreed. "It isn't. And I think the *Englischers* will agree."

"It isn't right for an Amish person to draw

too much attention," Eliza said. "All this—" she waved at the mosaics and paintings "—makes Sadie stand out too much."

Sadie's face tightened. "I don't sign my paintings. I make sure not to be prideful about it."

Katie nodded. "If anyone asks, we won't tell them who the artist is. We'll make sure not to put too much attention on you."

"*Danki*, Katie," Sadie said softly. "I don't want to be prideful. I just want to make the things that reflect what I feel inside."

"And I think that's why these will sell," Katie said. "You've poured your heart into them, and it shows."

Katie could only hope it would be enough to help save the shop that she had poured *her* heart into.

Gabriel had added a handful of his wood carvings to the display at the front of the shop, complementing Sadie's colorful artwork. By lunchtime, two wooden pigs and a painting had already sold. By closing, two mosaics, another painting and a wooden Christmas star had sold. Katie nearly danced back to the farmhouse that evening. She could not believe how well the plan was working. Levi saw the joy on her face, picked her up and spun her around the kitchen as they both laughed out loud with relief. Simon skipped around them in a circle, catching the excitement without knowing what they were excited about.

In addition to the brisk sales at the gift shop, the farm was running much more efficiently since Levi had implemented Katie's suggestions. She dared to believe it was only a matter of time before they could make enough to cover the back payments on the mortgage.

The days passed in rapid succession as Christmas grew near and people crowded shops throughout Bluebird Hills, eager to buy presents. The bell above the door of Aunt Fannie's Amish Gift Shop kept chiming as tourists hurried inside, bundled in coats and hats, eyes scanning the shelves for that perfect gift. Sadie struggled to keep up with demand and stayed up late each night, working by the light of a kerosene lantern to fill back orders. Katie went to bed exhausted but thrilled each evening.

Katie was eager to study the profits at the end of the week, but when she did, the numbers sent a cold jolt down her spine. She did the sums again and got the same results. They were selling nearly everything that Sadie made, and yet it still wasn't enough. Sales had picked up dramatically—but not enough to save the business.

By Christmas Eve, Katie had to face the truth.

Selling Sadie's art was a good idea, but it simply wasn't enough to save the shop. Along with the new marketing, it would have been enough to keep the business going successfully—if they weren't already in the hole. But that hole was just too deep to dig out of. She should have known that. The math had been there all along, laid out in cold, emotionless numbers in the ledger. But Katie had refused to believe it. She had been so desperate for her plan to work that she had ignored reality.

Katie knew she had to tell Levi. There was nothing left to do but accept the inevitable. Even if it broke both their hearts and made it impossible for them to be together.

Simon had been chattering nonstop for the last three days about his school's Christmas Eve program. "I have a really long line, *Daed*," he reminded his father the evening of the big event. "It's a lot of work to remember it all. But my friends are counting on me, so I can't let them down."

Levi tousled his son's hair and tried not to chuckle. "You won't let them down," he said. "You remember facts all the time. You're always telling me about the life cycle of the eastern salamander—"

"Eastern *newt, Daed*."

"See what I mean? You always know your stuff. So don't worry."

"*Ya*, but that's easy to remember."

"Tell me your lines. I bet you know them."

Levi gave a serous nod, cleared his throat and recited his part in a booming, monotone voice.

"You remembered perfectly," Levi said. "So no need to worry."

"Okay." Simon looked up at Levi solemnly. "Be sure not to tell Katie my line, okay? I want to surprise her."

Levi's heart warmed at the thought. "I'm sure she'll be very impressed."

Simon glanced at the battery clock ticking on the wall. "We better get going, *Daed*. The roads might be icy, and I don't want to be late." He adjusted his glasses while maintaining an earnest expression. "We need to allow extra time."

Levi chuckled at how much Simon sounded like a little adult. "*Gut* idea, *sohn*. I'll hitch up the buggy while you go tell Katie it's time to go."

"Sure thing, *Daed*!" Simon zipped out of the apartment, eyes glowing with excitement. His footsteps pounded down the steps hard enough to rattle the floor. If only Simon were so eager to get to school on time on regular school days, Levi thought with a smile.

He hurried into his coat and gloves and followed Simon down the stairs, through the shop and out into the blustery winter evening. Cold air stung his eyes as he led the horse from her stall to the buggy. After fastening the last buckle, he stomped his feet to stay warm as he waited for Katie and Simon to emerge from the farmhouse.

The door flew open and Simon burst outside, pulling Katie by one hand. She clasped a Tupperware container against her chest with the other hand. "All ready, *Daed*," Simon shouted as he galloped across the yard, tugging Katie behind him. "Let's go!"

Levi opened the buggy door for Katie and helped her into the seat, then tucked the lap robe around her.

"I hear Simon has a very important line," Katie said. "I can't wait to hear it."

Simon's face broke into an enormous grin. "It's a surprise."

The first stars twinkled on a purple horizon as the buggy rumbled toward the one-room schoolhouse. Christmas lights flicked on in *Englisch* farmyards along the roadside as darkness rolled in. Katie shivered and pulled the lap robe higher, until it covered her forearms.

"Too cold?" Levi asked with a frown.

"A little. But I know what will warm us up."

"Hot chocolate?" Simon asked hopefully from the back seat.

"Nee," Katie said. "I didn't have time to make us any for the road. I was going to say we can sing Christmas carols. That will warm us up."

"It will?" Simon asked, unconvinced.

"Sure will," Levi said. He took a deep breath and sang the first line of "Good King Wenceslas" in a rich, baritone voice. Katie met Levi's eyes, grinned and joined in with her clear, soft alto. Simon piped in from the back of the buggy, singing wildly off-key, as loudly as he could. "Hey," he said after the last line. "That worked! But only if you sing really loudly."

Katie and Levi both chuckled, then sang "It Came upon a Midnight Clear." The carol rang through the still, dark night all the way to the schoolhouse, where they arrived with ruddy cheeks and numb noses but warm inside their hearts.

Gray buggies lined the schoolyard and neighbors chatted with one another as they strode into the white clapboard building holding cake pans and tins of Christmas cookies. Levi took the plastic container from Katie to carry for her. While they walked, he snapped open the corner of the lid and peeked inside to see homemade peppermint bark. "Can't wait to dig into this," he said as they strolled through the open door.

"I made an extra batch for you and Simon. It's waiting for you at home."

"*Danki!* We'll make short work of it." It felt so good to have a woman in his life again, making treats just for him and his son.

The interior of the schoolhouse was noisy with the buzz of conversation and the laughter of children. A potbellied stove in the center of the room radiated heat throughout the small, crowded space. Levi wove through knots of people to lay the container on a long folding table beside the other holiday treats. Katie stayed by his side, but Simon disappeared and they lost sight of him. "He's so excited for the program to begin," Levi said. "He must be getting ready with the other *kinner.*"

"For sure and certain," Katie replied with a soft laugh. They saw Sadie and her family across the packed room and waved, then bumped into Gabriel and his aunt Mary and chatted with them until the program began.

When the time finally came for Simon to speak, Levi held his breath as he watched his skinny, solemn-looking son stare at the crowd through his thick glasses. Katie must have sensed Levi's anxiety—and been nervous herself—because her hand moved to his arm and squeezed gently.

Simon opened his mouth to speak, then paused to adjust his glasses. Levi leaned forward, heart pounding into his throat. Then

Simon spread his arms wide and announced in a dramatic voice, "The government shall be upon his shoulder: and his name shall be called Wonderful, Counselor, The mighty God, The everlasting Father, The Prince of Peace!"

Levi let out the breath he had been holding. Simon caught his eye, then Katie's, and beamed. Levi grinned back at his son. There was so much to be worried about right now—but inexplicably, deep in his heart, he suddenly felt like everything was going to be okay.

Following Amish tradition, Levi, Simon and Katie celebrated Christmas Day in prayer and quiet contemplation, solemnly reflecting on the significance of the holiday. That evening, they sat down to a feast of honey-baked ham, yeast rolls, stuffing, cranberry sauce, mashed potatoes, green beans, apple crumble and pumpkin pie. Having Katie at the table with him and Simon seemed like the only proper way to celebrate Christmas. Levi had trouble imagining the day without her, even though this was their first Christmas together.

After dinner, they cozied up in the living room to exchange gifts. Earlier in the week, Simon and Levi had decorated the windowsills with pine branches, pine cones and white candles. Levi lit the candle in each window before sitting down with a contented sigh. The tiny yellow flames glowed against the windowpanes, highlighting a swirl of white snowflakes behind the glass. Beyond lay darkness, but inside the farmhouse it was warm and snug.

Katie sat beside the fireplace, a green-and-red quilt tucked around her legs, the light from the flames highlighting her face. Levi studied her for a moment, feeling a sense of amazement that she was here, in his life, sharing this holy day with him and Simon. What had begun as a rivalry had somehow evolved into friendship and then, amazingly, deep affection. Gott *certainly does work in mysterious ways*, Levi thought.

"Time for presents!" Simon shouted, bouncing up and down on the sofa. "What's taking so long?"

"Just thinking about how blessed we are," Levi murmured with a quiet smile.

"Here," Katie said as she passed a brown paper package tied with string to Simon. "This one's from me."

He tore open the paper to reveal a hardcover book titled *Wildlife of Pennsylvania*. "Yes!" Simon whooped as he flipped open the cover to scan the photographs.

Levi exchanged a happy glance with Katie, but he caught something behind her smile that seemed distant and somber. His mood deflated a little as he wondered what was wrong. Didn't Katie want to be here as much as he wanted her here?

Simon hopped up from the sofa and launched himself at Katie. His small arms wrapped around her neck, and he clung to her as he whispered, "I'm so glad you came, Katie. I think my *mamm* would like you. I know my *daed* does." He pulled away and looked at Levi, then back to Katie with a serious expression. "I don't want anything to change. I like things the way they are right now, with Katie here. Everything feels *gut* now, doesn't it, *Daed*?"

Levi felt a lump in his throat as he answered hoarsely, "For sure and certain, *sohn*." He repeated the words for emphasis, slowly and thoughtfully. "For sure and certain."

Katie's face tightened, and she looked down. Levi felt his chest constrict along with her expression. Something was wrong. He knew there was the underlying uncertainty about the business, which would stress anyone out, but was there something else bothering her? Was she having second thoughts about their relationship? It wasn't like her to seem so distracted and distant.

"Sometimes things have to change," she murmured softly, eyes on her hands folded in her lap.

Simon didn't hear. He was too busy grabbing a gift from the coffee table and shaking it. But Levi heard, and the comment left him troubled. What did Katie know that she wasn't telling him?

Simon didn't give Levi time to brood. He shoved a present in Levi's lap and said, "Open this one first. I made it."

Levi unwrapped the brown paper to reveal a construction-paper bookmark. Simon had drawn the Christmas star on it in yellow crayon and tied a length of braided yellow yarn to the top. *"Danki, sohn,"* Levi said and caught Simon in a hug before he could scamper away to grab another present.

"I was going to add some sheep at the bottom, but the star took up too much room." Simon wiggled out of his father's tight embrace. "I hope you like it anyway."

"Of course I like it," Levi said. "It's perfect just like this."

Simon beamed and handed a cylinder-shaped package to Katie. "My teacher told everyone to make this for their *mamm*. You're not my *mamm*, but since I don't have one anymore, I thought you might like to be a *mamm* to me. I've never actually had one, you know. Not one that I can remember, anyway."

"Oh, Simon…" Tears welled in Katie's eyes. "That's a *wunderbaar* thing to hear."

Simon tilted his head. "Then why are you sad?"

"I'm not sad! I am so, so happy. I just have something in my eye, that's all." She swiped at her eyes, then tore the brown paper to reveal a coffee can covered in construction paper with snakes and lizards drawn on it. "You can put your big spoons and spatulas in," Simon said. "It goes on the kitchen counter. See, I covered the construction paper with contact paper so it's waterproof and will last a long time. I drew some of my favorite animals on it. Do you like it?"

"I love it!" Katie said. Fresh tears welled in her eyes. She turned her head and quickly dabbed them with her sleeve. When she looked back at them, her eyes were dry but red. She forced a wide grin. "Thank you so much, Simon. You can't imagine how much this means to me... All of it."

Levi felt like his heart would burst. He didn't have words for the emotions he felt as he watched his motherless son connect with the woman who had unexpectedly come into their lives. He savored the moment before pulling out a flat, square package from behind the sofa, where he had hidden it. "Look what I found for Katie," he said with a twinkle in his eye.

"Levi, you shouldn't have!" Katie exclaimed. But her face said otherwise.

"*Ach*, well, you don't even know if you'll like it."

"I'm sure I will." She ripped open the paper and gasped as she saw an oil painting depicting the gift shop, with the red barn, tall white silo and squat, round grain bin in the distance. The painting captured the scene in a swirl of cheerful colors.

Levi wanted Katie to feel seen and understood—that's why he had given her a gift that represented something dear to her heart. He leaned forward in his seat to watch Katie's reaction, eager to see the excitement on her face.

But instead of smiling, Katie's lip quivered. She looked like she was on the verge of tears again, but this time there was no joy shining in her eyes, as there had been with Simon's gift.

"I know it's fancy," Levi said quickly. "We won't hang it in the house, of course. It's for the shop. I thought it could go behind the counter, kind of like an advertisement. We can tell customers they can special order one from Sadie that depicts their own home. *Englischers* like that kind of thing. Could be really *gut* for business." Amish Christmas presents were usually predictable, practical and simple—a pair of mittens or a new casserole dish, for instance—but

Levi felt this gift was okay, even though it was a bit extravagant, since it was for the business.

Katie did not seem to understand that. Her face paled and her breath escaped in a strangled moan as she suddenly stood up and turned away. Levi realized that something was very, very wrong. "Simon," he said evenly, "why don't you take your new book into the kitchen and read it while you have some peppermint bark?"

"Oh, that sounds perfect!" Simon said, oblivious to Katie's distress. He bounced up from the couch, book pressed against his chest, and skipped out of the living room. The space sounded very quiet after he left. Levi could hear the tick of the battery-powered clock and the whisper of wind outside the windows. The fire crackled and popped in the fireplace. Katie's back was still turned, but her shoulders shook and her breath sounded harsh and uneven, so Levi knew she was crying. He stood and put a gentle hand on her shoulder. "Katie. What's wrong? What have I done? If it's the painting, we can get rid of it. I didn't mean to be too fancy."

Katie shook her head fiercely. "It's not the painting. I mean, it is, kind of. But not in the way that you think."

"Shh," Levi murmured. He put his other hand

on Katie's arm and slowly turned her to face him. "It's all right. I'm here."

"Nee," Katie said. A shudder ran through her. "It's not all right, because you won't be here. None of us will."

Katie collapsed against Levi's chest and let the tears flow freely. She could hear the beating of his heart beneath her cheek and feel the rhythmic rise and fall of his chest. The movement made her feel safe and grounded, even as their world was falling apart. She breathed in the woodsy scent that clung to him as she tightened her grip on his sleeves. She never wanted to let him go. She wanted to stay in his arms forever and never face the future.

"Shh," Levi murmured into her hair. He kissed the top of her prayer *kapp* and moved his hand over her back in big, soothing circles. "It's going to be *oll recht*."

Katie pulled back to look up into his eyes. "No, you don't understand." She fought back another sob. "I've run the numbers. We didn't make enough to pay off what we owe the bank in time. We did everything we could…" She shook her head. "But it wasn't enough. And there's nothing more we can do."

She waited for Levi's response. He said nothing, and she rested her cheek against his chest again. His hands kept moving over her back in soothing circles, as if he had forgotten to stop. "I'm sorry to ruin Christmas," Katie said, her face still pressed against his blue cotton shirt. "I tried to wait to tell you until tomorrow. But when I saw the painting...it broke my heart and I couldn't hold it in anymore." She swallowed hard. "The dream is gone, Levi."

"Gone?" Levi asked gently. "*Nee*, Katie. God knows the plans He has for us. This is not a surprise to Him."

Katie nodded into his chest, her tears dampening the cotton fabric of his shirt. "*Ya*, but..."

"Trust that this will work out for *gut*. Trust *Gott* to create a new dream for us."

Fresh tears welled in Katie's eyes. She wanted to run the gift shop and live in the farmhouse with Levi. She wanted it more than anything. Her life here had turned out better than she had ever dreamed it could have. "I know you're right, but it still hurts so much. How can you bear to lose your home, your business...everything?"

"Not everything, Katie." Levi's eyes were steady and firm on hers. "We still have each other." His gaze bored into her. "You're right, losing this place is going to hurt—it's going to hurt badly—but I know I can get through it, because—" Levi hesitated, then plunged ahead.

"Because I love you. And I think you love me, too."

"You…you love me?"

"*Ya*, Katie Schwartz. I love you."

Katie felt a new strength well up from deep within her. It spread from her belly to fill her chest and overflow outward, all the way to her fingertips and toes. "I love you, too, Levi Miller."

Levi leaned into her. She smelled his familiar masculine scent of leather and pine. Her heart skipped a beat as he drew closer, until she could feel his warm breath on her face.

And then he kissed her.

Katie melted into him. And when he leaned back from her to look into her eyes, she responded softly, "You are my new dream, Levi."

And she meant it with all her heart.

Chapter Twelve

The next morning, Katie woke without feeling dread for the future for the first time in weeks. She took a deep breath, stretched and exhaled. Eliza, Priss, Lovina, Gabriel and Mary would be coming over to celebrate Second Christmas, when Amish friends and families gathered to feast and celebrate the holiday together. Katie couldn't wait for the day to start.

Company began arriving soon after breakfast, cheeks red from cold, arms piled high with tins of Christmas cookies and casseroles. Katie and Levi greeted them all at the door and ushered them into the warm kitchen, where they gathered around the woodstove to drink *kaffi* and hot chocolate. Steam rose from the mugs to mingle with the scents of pine boughs and cinnamon rolls fresh from the oven.

"Where's Simon?" Priss asked as she tore apart a hot cinnamon roll.

"He was taking care of his pets when I left our apartment to come over here," Levi replied. "He should be here any minute."

Priss stuffed a big bite into her mouth, chewed, then said, "Mmm mmope eee murries."

The adults chuckled. "What was that?" Gabriel asked.

Priss swallowed and wiped her mouth with the back of a pudgy hand. "I hope he hurries." She licked sticky, sugary icing from her fingers and added, "Can we go on the hayride now? Please?"

Eliza frowned and shook her head. "There's too much snow out there to pull the wagon through the fields. We'll have to postpone until another time."

Priss's face fell. "But…" Her bottom lip began to tremble.

"Your *mamm*'s right," Levi said. "We can't pull the wagon. But we can pull a sleigh instead."

Eliza looked surprised. "You have a sleigh?"

"Not exactly." Levi rubbed the back of his neck sheepishly. "I knew how much the *kinner* were looking forward to the hayride today, so I came up with an alternative solution."

"That must be why I heard all that banging and clanging in the barn on Christmas Eve," Katie said.

"*Ya.* It's not exactly a sleigh, but I managed to put together something that should glide through the snow."

Katie put a hand on Levi's arm and squeezed. "The *kinner* will be so happy."

Priss jumped up and down, the remnants of the cinnamon roll still clutched in one hand. "Can we go right now? Please, please, please!"

"I don't see why not," Levi said with a grin. "If Eliza says its okay."

Eliza adjusted her glasses as she considered. "I guess it will be okay as long as you bundle up."

"I'll get the horse hitched up," Levi said as he reached for his coat and black felt hat. Gabriel followed Levi, blasting the warm room with frigid air when they opened the door.

The rest of the adults sorted through the winter clothing that hung on pegs by the kitchen door. Eliza helped her daughter into her coat, then draped a heavy kerchief over the girl's *kapp* and tied it snugly beneath her chin. "There. All set, ain't so?"

Priss tugged on her mittens and clapped her hands, even though the sound was muffled by the wool. "Ready to go!" she squealed.

They filed out the door into the clear, bright day, snug in their warm outerwear. Sunshine sparkled across the white landscape, creating a wonderland that seemed a world away from the muddy fields and gravel roads hidden beneath the snow. Katie felt a surge of excitement as the sun hit her face and the brisk air stung her cheeks. She was going to spend the day with the man she loved and the little boy who had chosen her as his new *mamm*, surrounded by friends who were quickly becoming family. Katie didn't know what would happen to them when the new year came, but she knew *Gott* did, and that was enough for today.

When they reached the barnyard, Katie laughed at the "sleigh" that Levi had hitched up to Old Gus. He had simply nailed some old sheets of plywood together to form a wide platform that would glide over the snow—in theory, at least.

"What do you think?" Levi asked. He held the horse's bridle and grinned at the group as they tramped through the snow toward him and Gabriel.

"I think it's going to be fun!" Katie said. "I'll race you," she shouted to Priss and Eliza, then took off through the deep drifts.

After a few strides, Katie's dress tangled around her legs and she collapsed into a snow bank. Priss shot past. "Beat you!" she shouted without slowing down.

Katie pulled herself to her feet and shook the

snow from the skirt of her emerald green cape dress.

"So did I," Eliza said with a wry smile as she trudged past Katie.

"I didn't expect that you would actually race me!" Katie said.

"It didn't take much effort."

Katie laughed. "Slow and steady wins the race, ain't so?"

"Are you calling me a turtle?" Eliza asked in a dry tone, but her eyes twinkled.

"Simon would call that a compliment," Katie said.

Eliza's attention darted to the windows above the shop. "Where *is* Simon? Shouldn't he be out here by now?"

Levi frowned and passed the reins to Gabriel. "*Ya.* I was just going to check on him. I'll be back with him by the time you get situated on the sleigh."

They piled onto the platform as Levi pushed through the unbroken snow to the apartment. Priss's elbow caught Katie's side, and she wiggled away, only to bump into Mary. Mary shifted backward, lost her balance and nearly fell off the sleigh. Gabriel caught her and helped her settle back into place. "Better cozy up," he said. "And hang on tight."

They were still trying to fit on the platform

and laughing at the ridiculousness of cramming too many adults into a tight space when Levi returned. Katie looked up at him, saw his expression, and her laughter cut off abruptly.

"Simon's not in the apartment," Levi said.

"But that's impossible," Katie said. She fumbled against Priss's back, leveraged herself up using Eliza's shoulder and rose to her feet. "He has to be here."

Levi spread his hands wide. "I know. It doesn't make any sense. He's not in the house, and he's not in the barn. So where else could he be?"

Katie felt a surge of protective energy pulse through her. "The grain bin," she said. "He was playing at the bottom of the ladder the other day. What if he went back this morning and…" The air surrounding the group tightened with fear.

"He wouldn't go in there," Gabriel said. "He knows how dangerous it is."

"What if he thought there was an animal in there that needed help?" Levi said. "*Gott* help us," he murmured as he turned on his heels and raced for the looming structure. They all knew how dangerous grain bins could be when filled with feed corn. If Simon climbed through the access door and fell into the grain, he might sink beneath the surface and be unable to breathe— like drowning on dry ground.

Gabriel hurried alongside Levi, their black coats and pants cutting a dark contrast against the white snow.

"He would know better than to go inside the grain bin when it's full of feed corn," Eliza said as they watched the two men run toward the imposing structure. But her pinched expression showed she wasn't convinced.

"Simon doesn't like to go into places like that," Priss said. "He'd rather read a book." She looked from one adult to the other, confused and scared at the sudden turn of events.

"Priss is right," Mary said. "But…" She cut her eyes to the little girl and closed her mouth into a tight line.

Katie shook her head. "No, it doesn't make sense. I can't believe it." *I won't believe it*, she thought. "He could have wandered off anywhere. Once Levi checks the grain bin, we'll need to keep looking." No one added, *if he isn't in the bin*. Their bleak faces spoke the words for them. "Let's just go ahead and start looking now," Katie added. "I can't sit here waiting. I'll check the barn again. Maybe he's in the hayloft and Levi missed him when he hitched up Old Gus."

"I'll search by the road," Lovina said. She turned to her granddaughter with a no-nonsense expression. "Priss, take Eliza to all the places you and Levi like to play when you're outside."

"Mary, please stay near the house in case he comes back," Katie added. "Shout for us if you see him."

Katie tore through the barn, shouting Simon's name. Her pulse drummed in her ears as she climbed into the hayloft and glanced around. He wasn't there. She scrambled back down the rough wooden ladder, searched the tack room and rushed outside again. Levi was jogging back from the grain bin. "It's okay," he shouted. "The door was secure. He couldn't have gotten in."

"Thank You, *Gott*," Katie whispered.

"Gabriel's going to search the bottom field," Levi said.

"And we've split up to search the farmyard," Katie said.

Levi took off his black felt hat and ran his fingers through his hair. "I just don't understand. This isn't like Simon. He doesn't wander off. And he would never miss this sleigh ride. He's been talking about it all week." Levi stopped talking suddenly, and his face drained of color. "You don't think…" He looked at Katie with wide, fearful eyes.

"Talk to me, Levi. What is it?"

"That day I worked in the shop, a little girl refused to speak to me because she wasn't allowed to talk to strangers. It just hit me. What if…" Levi swallowed hard, unable to say the dreaded words.

"Nee," Katie said firmly. She placed her hands on each of his cheeks and gently tilted his face downward, forcing him to focus on her. "Look at me. Nobody has kidnapped Simon. He's okay. And we *will* find him."

Levi exhaled sharply. Then he grabbed Katie and pulled her against him in a fierce hug. "Don't you ever leave me, Katie Schwartz," he said into her hair, arms locked around her slender frame, his body trembling against hers from cold and adrenaline. "I told you that I love you, but I didn't tell you that I *need* you." His warm breath rasped against her ear. "I've been on my own for so long. I thought I could handle everything all by myself. That's what men are supposed to do, ain't so? But I can't. And since I met you, I don't want to."

"I don't want to, either," she whispered. "I don't want to be strong all the time."

Levi squeezed her, then released her and stepped back. He nodded, then swallowed hard. "Let's go find Simon."

Levi and Katie took the buggy to search the plowed roads leading north of the property, while Lovina drove her buggy in the opposite direction. The others continued searching the grounds. Before they pulled out of the gravel drive, Mary grabbed Biscuit's bridle and told them she was going to run over to Sadie's house and ask her family to help, too. Then she let go, gave the horse a solid pat on the rump, and the buggy jerked forward.

Levi had to drive slowly to keep Biscuit's hooves from slipping in the snow and ice. "Easy now," he murmured as she fought the bit and tossed her head. The slow pace made the journey even more stressful. Levi strained his eyes, searching the fields and pastures alongside the road, hoping and praying to see a small silhouette trudging through the snowdrifts.

After a long, tense time—how long, he didn't know—Levi saw a figure standing by the road in the distance, and his heart leaped into his throat. But he quickly realized it was only a snowman wearing an old hat and a threadbare scarf. It took a long time for his heart to settle back into its regular rhythm.

The buggy wheels ground through the snow as Levi hunched his shoulders against the cold, eyes burning from staring for too long. And then he glimpsed a small, dark silhouette in the distance. A blue object swept behind the figure. He squinted, straining to make out what it might be.

"Over there, Levi," Katie said with a tremor in her voice. "Could it be…?"

"*Ya*, I see it, too." Levi swallowed hard and studied the figure. "It's a boy, all right. But is it Simon?"

Katie straightened in her seat and shielded her eyes from the sun that beat down on the snow and danced off the ice crystals. "What's he dragging behind him?"

They both leaned forward, jaws tight with tension as they drew closer and the image slowly became clearer.

"It's a sled!" Katie said as the object sharpened into focus.

"And it *is* Simon!" Levi recognized his skinny silhouette and loping gait. "I know it is!"

"*Ya*," Katie said, breaking into an enormous grin. "I know it is, too!"

Levi felt a massive weight lift from his shoulders. Suddenly his world was all right again. "Simon!" he shouted. The boy's head swiveled toward them, and he looked surprised. He stopped walking and scratched his bony elbow. He watched as the buggy approached, Biscuit's hooves crunching against the snow in a steady rhythm.

"What's that on the sled he's been dragging behind him?" Levi wondered aloud.

"It looks like..." Katie gasped. "Why, it's all his pets! He's got all their cages stacked on the sled."

Levi shook his head. "What on earth?"

Simon offered a sheepish wave and a weak smile as they pulled onto the shoulder. "Whoa, girl." Levi tugged the reins, then tossed them to Katie and jumped from the buggy before it came to a full stop. He cut the distance to his son in four quick steps, fell to one knee and wrapped his arms around the boy.

"What's the matter, *Daed*?" Simon asked in a small, earnest voice.

Levi pulled back and looked directly into Simon's eyes. "You've scared us all half to death, that's what! Don't you ever run away like this again!" Levi's voice rose as the words poured out of him, until he was booming at Simon, his brows pulled together in a fierce frown. "Just what do you think you're doing?"

Simon's bottom lip began to wobble as he stared into his father's eyes. "I... I...was..." A tear trickled down his cheek.

"What, Simon? What did you think you were doing?"

"Levi," Katie said quietly but firmly.

Simon flinched as her voice pulled him back from his emotions and he realized that he had been shouting. His eyes darted to her, and she shook her head. Levi turned back to Simon. "I'm sorry," he said in a soft voice. "I shouldn't have shouted at you. I was just so scared..."

Simon hiccuped and wiped his eyes with the back of his woolen mitten. "I was trying to help."

"I don't understand," Levi murmured.

"I overheard what Katie told you last night about losing our home," Simon said.

"So you ran away?" Levi looked at Simon incredulously.

"*Nee*. I'm not running away. I'm earning money to save the farm."

"What?" Levi glanced at Katie. She was biting her lip as tears welled in her eyes. Levi turned back to Simon. "What were you planning to do to earn this money?"

"I'm headed to the Bluebird Hills Zoo to sell my pets. Then I'll give you the money and you can pay off the bank."

"Oh, Simon." Levi didn't know what to say. His heart overflowed with an overwhelming mix of love, relief and sadness. "You would sacrifice your pets that you love so much?"

"For our family? *Ya*." Simon stared at Levi through his thick glasses with big, solemn eyes.

"*Sohn*, I am so sorry I yelled at you when you were only trying to help by giving away what you love most."

Simon looked surprised. His forehead crinkled. "Not what I love most, *Daed*. I love *you* most." His eyes darted to Katie. "And Katie, too. I want us to be a family and live together in our farmhouse."

Levi felt a sob rising from deep within. He pushed it down, but moisture still filled his eyes. He pulled Simon into a tight hug before his son could see the tears. "I'm sorry, Simon. But selling your pets won't earn enough money. And the zoo wouldn't buy them, anyway."

"Oh." Levi felt Simon's body sag. "I thought I could save our home."

Levi let out a long, slow breath. "We all tried our best, *sohn*. But we have to leave it to *Gott* now."

"I don't want to move."

"I know, *sohn*, none of us do. But you'll get to keep your pets, at least. That's something, ain't so?"

Simon swallowed hard and nodded. "*Ya.* I was real sad to sell Oscar and Simon Jr."

Levi's heart warmed, even in the midst of heartbreak, at his son's sweet nature. "Now what do you say we head back to the house? We can have that sleigh ride you've been so excited about."

"Okay, *Daed.*"

Levi released Simon from the hug and stood up. He brushed the snow from his knee with one hand while Simon slipped his small fingers into the other. "You know, *Daed*, I'm glad you found me. I was getting pretty cold, and my feet were hurting. And I was kind of lost. Good thing I put the battery powered heater in the wagon to keep my pets warm."

Levi didn't tell Simon that he was miles from Bluebird Hill's small, locally owned zoo—or that he had been heading in the wrong direction. He just squeezed the boy's hand. "I'm glad I found you, too. And I'm not angry with you anymore. But you have to understand that you can't leave like this again. You could get hurt. Especially when it's cold."

"Okay, *Daed*. I'll tell you my plan next time. I just didn't want you to stop me." He looked up at Levi. "I really thought it would work and you and Katie would be proud of me."

Levi stopped walking and gazed into his son's warm brown eyes. "I couldn't be prouder of you than I am right now, Simon."

Everyone was elated when they returned home. The search was called off, and they gathered in the living room to warm up by the fireplace with slices of hot apple pie. Soon Simon and Priss scampered off to play, and all the adults turned to Levi and Katie with questioning looks. Lovina was the first to say it out loud. "What we don't understand is why Simon would run off like that with all his pets. It doesn't make any sense. And today of all days!"

Katie and Levi exchanged a pained look. They couldn't keep their financial situation a secret any longer. Levi explained quickly, eyes on his empty plate. When he finished, the room was silent. The *kinner*'s voices drifted through the ceiling from the upstairs bedroom. Outside, a bird chirped from the feeder hanging by the front porch. Levi looked up, expecting to see disappointed faces full of reprimand for his failure.

Instead, every expression in the room was of concern and compassion, not condemnation. Lovina frowned and stepped forward. "Well, this won't do."

Levi shrugged. "There's nothing to be done about it."

Lovina raised an eyebrow. "I wouldn't be so sure about that." She and Eliza exchanged a look. Eliza nodded slightly and pushed her glasses up the bridge of her nose. "You leave it to us."

"*Nee*, we've done everything we could. Eliza and Gabriel, I'm so sorry that you'll lose your jobs. Maybe whoever buys this place will keep you on…"

Lovina clicked her tongue. "You shouldn't have kept this from us. We could have been working together this whole time to find a solution."

"I didn't want…" Levi wasn't sure how to finish that sentence.

"We thought we could handle it ourselves," Katie cut in. "We thought we could stay in control that way." She gave a wry laugh. "It didn't work."

"Well, I'm going to do what you should have done a long time ago," Lovina said with a sniff. "I'm going to bring the community together and find a way through this. That's what we're here for, ain't so? That's what makes us Amish."

Two weeks later, Katie could hardly believe what she was seeing. The field behind the gift shop was filled with parked buggies and *Englisch* cars as people flooded in to bid at the community-wide auction Lovina and Eliza had organized. Amish families throughout the church district had donated goods and services to auction off, with all the proceeds going to save the Miller-Schwartz property. Men with long beards and wearing black coats and black felt hats, women wearing cape dresses and *kapps*, and people wearing fancy *Englisch* clothing and jewelry filled the barn and farmyard. "We came all the way from North Carolina," Katie overheard a woman in a pink dress and knee-high brown boots say as she slid out of her silver minivan. "I hear this is *the* place to get authentic Amish furniture this year."

Furniture, quilts, canned goods, crafts and even livestock—the outpouring of donations was overwhelming. Lovina winked as she strode by, Eliza following close behind with a yellow notepad and pencil in hand. Eliza stopped and turned to Levi and Katie. "We've already earned enough," she said and tapped a row of numbers on the pad with the pencil.

"You mean…" Katie and Levi looked at one another, then back at Eliza.

Eliza nodded. "Yep. We've got enough to pay off the debt and save the property."

Katie was so thrilled she was beyond words. She could only stand there, feeling a flood of joy so deep it made her close her eyes and thank *Gott*.

"We get to stay?" Simon asked, eyes big with hope through his thick glasses.

"*Ya*, you do."

Simon whooped and jumped into the air.

Eliza tapped the notepad again. "And I get to keep my job. It's a happy ending for us all. Now I'm off to check on that calf for sale. Looks like it needed some fresh water." *Leave it to dear Eliza to be so no-nonsense about such big news and just get on with it*, Katie thought.

Simon tugged Katie's hand and pointed to the dessert table. "Look at all the whoopie pies! Can I have one to celebrate?" The church district's women had held a work frolic to bake sweets to sell at the event, and, judging by the line of *Englischers* waiting to buy, sales were brisk.

"Sadie set aside a couple whoopie pies for you and Priss," Katie said.

"All right!" he shouted and pumped his fist in the air.

Levi chuckled. "Just stay where we can see you."

"Don't worry, *Daed*. I'm not going to get lost ever again." He gave Levi a big hug before scampering over to the dessert table, where Sadie waited with a smile on her face.

"Can you believe this?" Katie asked Levi as she surveyed the bustling crowd around them. "All this for us."

Levi shook his head. "It's such *gut* news, I don't think it's even hit me yet." He shook his head again. "We never should have tried to handle things by ourselves."

"Nee," Katie said. "Back in Indiana, when no one else stepped up to deal with the daily stress of *Mamm*'s illness, I eventually stopped asking for help. I got used to doing it all on my own until I relied only on myself."

"Ya." Levi exhaled. "After Rachel died and

then my sister moved away from Bluebird Hills to marry, I wanted to be strong and independent—to be everything Simon needed, since he didn't have a *mamm*. Somewhere along the way, I forgot that *Gott* gave us a community for a reason."

Levi turned abruptly toward Katie, his dark eyes suddenly serious. "And He gave me *you* for a reason."

Katie felt a shiver go down her spine. She could sense what Levi was about to say. Her lips parted with expectation as she gazed up into his eyes.

"I know it isn't the most romantic setting." Levi broke into a little half smile. "Okay, it's not a romantic setting at all. But, uh…" He cleared his throat and rubbed the back of his neck. "Well, I've been wanting to ask you something for a long time. But when we were going to lose our home and livelihood, I didn't feel like I had that right—not when I couldn't support a family. The thing is…would you…" He shifted his weight from one foot to the other.

"Levi Miller—the man who teased me mercilessly when we first met—is now somehow at a loss for words?"

Levi gave a goofy grin. "For sure and certain."

Katie returned the grin. "Then I'll help you out. Yes, Levi. I'll marry you."

"You knew what I was going to ask?"

"Of course I did."

Levi's face brightened. "And you said yes."

"I would have said yes even when we didn't know what the future held. I would have gone with you anywhere."

"And I would have gone anywhere with you, Katie Schwartz."

"It'll be Katie Miller soon," she said, saying the name aloud to see how it sounded.

"Can't happen soon enough."

"Agreed."

"Huh. A few months ago, I never thought I'd hear you agree with me." They both laughed as Levi slipped his hand in hers. The crowd wove around them, friendly voices shouted to friends and children darted past. "Nothing is like I planned or expected," Levi said. "Not even this proposal."

"Nee," Katie said as she clung to Levi's hand and gazed into his eyes. "It all turned out better than you or I could have ever planned."

Epilogue

The Lapp farmhouse was packed full of men and women in their best-for-church clothes. Katie peered over the rows of black felt hats and heart-shaped white *kapps* until her eyes landed on Sadie and Eliza. Sadie winked and flashed a wide grin. Eliza gave a nod of approval. Simon sat between them, bursting with barely contained excitement.

Katie couldn't believe the moment was finally here—after all the competition and strife, she and Levi stood in front of the entire congregation, ready to say their vows. Her heart flip-flopped into her throat as she turned her attention to the man she loved.

"Ready?" Levi mouthed.

"For sure and certain," Katie whispered.

Bishop Amos gave a wry smile and shook his head. "You two have come a long way since the first day you met."

Soft laughter rippled through the congregation.

"But I recognized something between you right away. That's when I realized Fannie had a matchmaking plan. She knew both of you well enough to understand that you were perfect for one another—even if it took you a while to figure that out for yourselves."

Another wave of laughter swept through the room, louder this time than before.

"You two had your own plans for your lives—but *Gott* had other ideas." Amos's eye twinkled just like it had when he first told Katie that she might be surprised how things turned out in the end.

"Thank *Gott* I didn't get what I thought I wanted," Levi said. He reached for Katie's hand and slipped his warm, callused fingers around hers. "I got something better than I ever knew to ask for."

Katie thought she would burst with joy as she stood beside the man she loved in front of a room full of friends who had become as close as family.

"So did I," Katie said, her eyes locked on Levi's.

Katie knew she was finally home.

And that home was not just a place called Bluebird Hills. It was a man who had unexpectedly stolen her heart.

* * * * *

Dear Reader,

Welcome to Bluebird Hills! I'm so glad you stopped by for a visit. When creating a new series, I always focus on building a world that feels inviting. This welcoming rural community in Pennsylvania's Amish country has all the elements that make me feel at home: small family farms with red barns, rambling clapboard farmhouses, gently rolling hills, a quaint main street with old-fashioned shops and tight-knit residents with colorful personalities. Be sure to look for the next Bluebird Hills installment, where quirky supporting characters from book one will become the heroes and heroines. I can't wait to share their stories with you.

This story is about the unwanted surprises that God sometimes sends our way. Katie and Levi, like so many of us, would rather their lives go according to their own plans. But the only way to find the blessing God intends for them is to give up control and go where He leads... I can certainly relate to Katie's and Levi's predicament. I love being in control (who doesn't?) but have learned that letting go leads to some of life's greatest and most fulfilling adventures.

Wishing you the best on whatever adventure

God is currently taking you on, and I look forward to seeing you again in Bluebird Hills. In the meantime, you can find me at virginiawisebooks.com, Facebook @VirginiaWiseBooks and Instagram @virginiawisebooks.

Love always,
Virginia Wise

COUNTRY LEGACY COLLECTION

19 FREE BOOKS IN ALL!

Cowboys, adventure and romance await you in this new collection! Enjoy superb reading all year long with books by bestselling authors like Diana Palmer, Sasha Summers and Marie Ferrarella!